LOUIS B. WRIGHT, General Editor. Director of the Folger Shakespeare Library from 1948 until his retirement in 1968, Dr. Wright has devoted over forty years to the study of the Shakespearean period. In 1926 he completed his doctoral thesis on "Vaudeville Elements in Elizabethan Drama" and subsequently published many articles on the stagecraft and theatre of Shakespeare's day. He is the author of *Middle-Class Culture in Elizabethan England* (1935), *Religion and Empire* (1942), *The Elizabethans' America* (1965), and many other books and essays on the history and literature of the Tudor and Stuart periods, including *Shakespeare for Everyman* (1964). Dr. Wright has taught at the universities of North Carolina, California at Los Angeles, Michigan, Minnesota, and other American institutions. From 1932 to 1948 he was instrumental in developing the research program of the Henry E. Huntington Library and Art Gallery. During his tenure as Director, the Folger Shakespeare Library became one of the leading research institutions of the world for the study of the backgrounds of Anglo-American civilization.

VIRGINIA A. LaMAR, Assistant Editor. A member of the staff of the Folger Shakespeare Library from 1946 until her death in 1968, Miss LaMar served as research assistant to the Director and as Executive Secretary. Prior to 1946 Miss LaMar had been a secretary in the British Admiralty Delegation in Washington, D.C., receiving the King's Medal in 1945 for her services. She was coeditor of the *Historie of Travell into Virginia Britania* by William Strachey, published by The Hakluyt Society in 1953, and author of *English Dress in the Age of Shakespeare* and *Travel and Roads in England* in the "Folger Booklets on Tudor and Stuart Civilization" series.

The Folger Library General Reader's Shakespeare

THE TRAGEDY OF
CORIOLANUS

by

WILLIAM
SHAKESPEARE

WASHINGTON SQUARE PRESS
PUBLISHED BY POCKET BOOKS NEW YORK

A Washington Square Press Publication of
POCKET BOOKS, a division of Simon & Schuster, Inc.
1230 Avenue of the Americas, New York, N.Y. 10020

ISBN: 0-671-49966-1

First Pocket Books printing April, 1962

10 9 8 7 6

Preface

This edition of *Coriolanus* is designed to make available a readable text of one of Shakespeare's less familiar plays. In the centuries since Shakespeare many changes have occurred in the meanings of words, and some clarification of Shakespeare's vocabulary may be helpful. To provide the reader with necessary notes in the most accessible format, we have placed them on the pages facing the text that they explain. We have tried to make these notes as brief and simple as possible. Preliminary to the text we have also included a brief statement of essential information about Shakespeare and his stage. Readers desiring more detailed information should refer to the books suggested in the references, and if still further information is needed, the bibliographies in those books will provide the necessary clues to the literature of the subject.

The early texts of all of Shakespeare's plays provide only inadequate stage directions, and it is conventional for modern editors to add many that clarify the action. Such additions, and additions to entrances, are placed in square brackets.

All illustrations are from material in the Folger Library collections.

L. B. W.
V. A. L.

September 20, 1961

The Perversity of Pride

Coriolanus is the last tragedy that Shakespeare wrote. Although there is little evidence to date it accurately, scholars generally agree that it was probably acted about 1607–1608, which would make it follow *Antony and Cleopatra*, that other Roman tragedy with a protagonist who has troubled critics and commentators as Coriolanus troubles them. The interpretations of Shakespeare's purpose and intention in *Coriolanus* have been varied and sometimes diametrically opposite. Some critics have seen the play as antidemocratic, an aristocratic condemnation of the rabble populace; others have interpreted it as a revelation of the evils of dictators and fascists. To some it is a political tract with overtones from events in Shakespeare's day; a few have seen in the character of Coriolanus reflections of Sir Walter Raleigh or the Earl of Essex; still others deny any political purpose at all.

Critics have been equally divided about the quality of the drama. To one it is evidence that Shakespeare had exhausted the tragic vein in a play that shows a flagging of his dramatic art. To others, including Mr. T. S. Eliot, it is Shakespeare's "most assured artistic success." Sir Edmund Chambers comments that "For the first time since some of the painful humors and strained wit-combats of his early experiments, Shakespeare has become tedious. Perhaps that is why the schoolmasters are so fond of the play."

The play is puzzling in its meaning and often compact and elliptical in its expression. It does offer an opportunity, as Chambers implies, for critical speculation that delights the heart of academics, especially those who like to read esoteric meanings into cloudy passages.

But to interpret *Coriolanus* as an obscure and mediocre play, turned out as a perfunctory theatrical piece because Shakespeare's company wanted a classical tragedy at the moment, is to do less than justice to both Shakespeare and the drama itself. Shakespeare knew what he was about, and the play does not "want art," as Ben Jonson might have said of it. In *Antony and Cleopatra* Shakespeare studied in dramatic terms a great character who allowed pleasure and sensuality to encompass his ruin; so in *Coriolanus* he focuses upon a noble character who lets pride and a perverted sense of honor destroy him.

The theme of honor was popular in the Renaissance, which produced countless discussions of this virtue and its place in the life of a gentleman. The Renaissance man was expected to strive for honor and fame. One of the most persistent themes in Italian poetry and in the courtesy books is the exhortation to seek honor, glory, fame. English writers took over the concept, which became part of the ethical motivation of the aristocratic group. Mr. Curtis B. Watson in *Shakespeare and the Renaissance Concept of Honor* observes: "For the Renaissance aristocracy, honor, good name, credit, reputation, and glory come close to the very center of their ethical values and receive expression almost wherever we look in the records of the nobility of that age. For this class, these values are so popular, so widespread, so trite, that they pass into its literature almost without definition, particularly into the drama of the age" [pp. 63–4].

In *Coriolanus* we have a hero whose overweening pride in his honor determines his attitude toward every action. He is a brave soldier who risks his life in battle for Rome, but one gets the impression that he is thinking less of Rome than of the glory accruing to himself. Though he deprecates the praise that his colleagues bestow upon him for his part in the victory over the Volsces, he is fully conscious of his worth and the fame that he has won. Even in his seemingly modest deprecation, he shows a resentment that anyone should assume the right to evaluate his conduct. Volumnia, his mother, who shares his feelings and indeed had formed those attitudes in Coriolanus from his infancy, tells Virgilia, his wife, "If my son were my husband, I should freelier rejoice in that absence wherein he won honor than in the embracements of his bed where he would show most love." [I. iii., ll. 2–5].

Coriolanus' pride in his position as the first of the patricians of Rome, his sense of honor that will not permit him to demean himself by seeking the favor of anyone, much less the favor of the sweaty populace, makes utterly abhorrent the thought of dressing in a gown of humility and begging the people for their suffrage. Only the utmost persuasion of his mother and his patrician colleagues can bring him to that sorry pass. When he finally appears before the plebeians, led like a balky horse by Menenius, he can hardly forbear to insult the garlic-breathed crowd:

> What must I say?
> "I pray, sir"—Plague upon't! I cannot bring
> My tongue to such a pace. "Look, sir, my wounds!
> I got them in my country's service, when
> Some certain of your brethren roared and ran
> From the noise of our own drums"
>   [II. iii., ll. 51–5].

When Coriolanus at length grudgingly asks a few citizens for their vote and is told by Sicinius the tribune that he has fulfilled the requirements and can remove the gown of humility, he comments:

> That I'll straight do, and, *knowing myself again,*
> Repair to the Senate House [II. iii., ll. 154–56].

Not for the consulship, nor to please his fellow senators, can Coriolanus masquerade for long as a politician.

From this point onward the spectator is aware that Coriolanus' haughty pride will never let him compromise with the realities of Roman politics. Inexorably it drives him to insult the tribunes and to scorn the plebeians until they in fury force his exile. To revenge himself upon a populace whom he considers an ingrate mob, he is ready to betray Rome to the Volsces. In the end, however, his innate nobility comes to the fore and he yields to the pleas of Volumnia with full knowledge that his action will alienate the Volsces and make certain his death at their hands. The denouement comes characteristically with Coriolanus' rage when Aufidius touches his pride by taunting him with weakness. By boasting of his deeds against the Corioli, Coriolanus arouses the hostility of the crowd and precipitates the melee in which the conspirators assassinate him. He dies as he had lived—the victim of his pride.

This is not a hero with whom the modern audience finds much to sympathize or in whom there is much to admire. Most of us may share his contempt for demagogues like Brutus and Sicinius, but that does not mean that we can identify ourselves with Coriolanus. Nevertheless, the protagonist in this play does provide a subject for the kind of morbid analysis that is popular today. It was the study of Coriolanus as a special type who was a prey to egotism and pride that must have fascinated his creator.

Shakespeare in *Coriolanus* does not write with the lyric quality of the earlier tragedies nor does he concern himself with the great cosmic verities that move him in such plays as *King Lear* and *Hamlet*. *Coriolanus* he wrote on another level in a different key, but that is not to say he failed to provide flashes of great poetry and shrewd insights into the nature of man. Nor does he neglect to people his stage with characters of flesh and blood. Even if one grants that *Coriolanus* shows a falling off in Shakespeare's art, there is no evidence here of Shakespeare's neglect of his theatrical craft.

Shakespeare always manages to give reality to his mob scenes, and in *Coriolanus* the plebeians behave and talk like disgruntled and angry commoners such as one has met before on Shakespeare's stage. The tribunes of the people, Brutus and Sicinius, are characteristic demagogues with a verisimilitude that makes them familiar to us as they were familiar to Shakespeare's contemporaries and indeed to all ages. Shakespeare distrusted the populace, perhaps as much as Alexander Hamilton distrusted it, but he treated it with humor and not with bitterness. The invectives that Coriolanus lavished upon the plebeians are not the expression of the author's own feelings. He had too much humanity—and too great a sense of the incongruous and the comic—to hate these people who were the victims of their own volatile emotions. The individual plebeians Shakespeare treats as decent human beings, but he shows that in the mass they are easily misled by politicians. In this play the plebeians can almost be considered a single character serving collectively as a counterfoil to Coriolanus.

In Menenius Shakespeare created a type always popular on the stage, the humorous old man with the foibles and vanities that give an opportunity for a good character actor to emphasize the comic elements. Like Polonius, Menenius is worldly-wise and fancies himself a *bon viveur* as well as a diplomat and statesman. Like Falstaff also, he goes out to demonstrate his power and influence with his former hail fellow, and like Falstaff he suffers the same kind of dramatic rejection. In Volumnia Shakespeare created a powerful character, the fabled Roman matron ready to suppress all softness and tenderness in driving her son to seek honor above everything else. In the end she is willing to sacrifice both son and herself to save Rome. Virgilia, the wife, though overshadowed by the formidable figure of her mother-in-law, is portrayed with care as a loving, devoted, and perhaps realistic wife, quite incapable of comprehending the high-flown sentiments of Volumnia on the subject of honor.

Perhaps Shakespeare is as bored as Virgilia with all the ranting about honor. Earlier he had had something to say about it in *Henry IV, Part 1,* where he let Hotspur make an oration:

By heaven, methinks it were an easy leap
To pluck bright honor from the pale-faced moon,
Or dive into the bottom of the deep,
Where fathom line could never touch the ground,
And pluck up drowned honor by the locks,

So he that doth redeem her thence might wear
Without corrival all her dignities

> [I. iii., ll. 211–17].

But later Falstaff, as he contemplates heroic death, gives a homespun and realistic commentary that might express the hidden feelings of Virgilia—and many in the audience at the performance of *Coriolanus*—over the high-flown sentiments of Volumnia and her son:

'Tis not due yet: I would be loath to pay him before his day. What need I be so forward with him that calls not on me? Well, 'tis no matter; honor pricks me on. Yea, but how if honor prick me off when I come on? How then? Can honor set to a leg? No. Or an arm? No. Or take away the grief of a wound? No. Honor hath no skill in surgery then? No. What is honor? A word. What is in that word honor? What is that honor? Air—a trim reckoning! Who hath it? He that died a Wednesday. Doth he feel it? No. Doth he hear it? No. 'Tis insensible then? Yea, to the dead. But will it not live with the living? No. Why? Detraction will not suffer it. Therefore I'll none of it. Honor is a mere scutcheon—and so ends my catechism.

> [V. i., ll. 129–43]

Shakespeare in *Coriolanus*, as elsewhere in his dramas, shows the common sense of the pragmatic Englishman of the Tudor and Stuart age. Many ideas and sentiments in the play reflect the attitudes and thinking of Shakespeare's contemporaries. For example, one of the most widely accepted social doctrines was the idea of degree in society which Menenius emphasized at the very beginning of the play with his fable of the rebellion of all the body's members against the belly. Shakespeare's placement of this fable in Act I, Scene 1 was deliberate, for it was to provide a significant theme in the forthcoming action.

Englishmen were fearful of civil disturbance. The memories of men were long and they recalled the commotions that had racked the state before the strong arms of the Tudors had brought stability; more recently they remembered the fear of civil strife when the great queen lay dying and the uncertainty of the succession brought sleepless nights to many of both high and low estate. The official homilies of the Established Church thundered against the iniquity of rebellion, and preachers in their pulpits constantly stressed the duty of subjects to remain peaceably in that station to which God had called them. Shakespeare himself earlier in *Troilus and Cressida* had placed in the mouth of Ulysses a moving speech on the necessity of degree:

The heavens themselves, the planets and this center
Observe degree, priority, and place.

. . . .

But when the planets
In evil mixture to disorder wander,

> What plagues and what portents! what mutiny!
> What raging of the sea! shaking of earth!
> Commotion in the winds! frights, changes, horrors,
> Divert and crack, rend and deracinate
> The unity and married calm of states
> Quite from their fixture! O, when degree is shaked,
> Which is the ladder of all high designs,
> The enterprise is sick! How could communities,
> Degrees in schools and brotherhoods in cities,
> Peaceful commerce from dividable shores,
> The primogenitive and due of birth,
> Prerogative of age, crowns, scepters, laurels,
> But by degree, stand in authentic place?
> Take but degree away, untune that string,
> And, hark, what discord follows [I. iii., ll. 85–110].

This doctrine was almost universally accepted by Englishmen and few would gainsay its validity. Garrulous old Menenius with his fable, which was as old as Plutarch but which Shakespeare could also have read in William Camden's *Remains* (1605), merely drove home a moral that would cause everyone in the audience, regardless of status, to nod his head in agreement.

Mr. J. B. Priestley in an informal talk before the Shakespeare Conference at Stratford-upon-Avon on August 28, 1961, commented upon a quality in Shakespeare of reflecting the views of the average Englishman. One remark has pertinence to *Coriolanus*. "The Englishman is at heart a snob," Mr. Priestley observed. "It is a trait that runs through the English from top to bottom. Shakespeare was a characteristic Englishman in this respect. Shakespeare distrusted the faceless, nameless mass—the mob." In *Coriolanus*, Shakespeare is not glorifying a dictator who can control the masses; indeed, if anything, he emphasized the folly of Coriolanus' actions. Nor is he an opponent of democracy—something neither he nor his contemporaries knew or dreamed of. He merely reflected the Englishman's distrust, as Mr. Priestley points out, of mobocracy.

SOURCE, TEXT, AND STAGE HISTORY

Shakespeare used for his plot Plutarch's "Life of Coriolanus" in North's translation of *The Lives of the Noble Grecians and Romans*. Plutarch understandably gives less reality to this life than to the other more historical characters in his parallel lives, for Coriolanus is a mythical figure from the dim and misty past of Roman legend. He belongs in that category of semihistorical characters that include Cymbeline and King Lear. Shakespeare followed the main outlines as he found them in Plutarch and in some instances took over North's phraseology, but he deleted incidents that were not pertinent to his dramatic presentation and altered others to suit his purposes. For example, Shakespeare took a rather wooden and insignificant Menenius in Plutarch and made a lifelike and important character out of him. Volumnia he also developed far beyond Plutarch's conception. He likewise built up Aufidius to make him a worthy opponent of Coriolanus. A study of the deletions and amplifications of his Plutarchan source offers an instructive lesson in the way a practical playwright like Shakespeare changed prose to poetical drama.

The story of Coriolanus was not unknown to Elizabethans, for it had appeared in William Painter's *The Palace of Pleasure* (1566–1567), which Shakespeare knew. But the fuller story as found in North's Plutarch made it unnecessary for him to use Painter.

The text of *Coriolanus* is based on that in the First Folio of 1623, for there was no earlier quarto version. Copy for the text used by the printers of the First Folio, many scholars believe, was a carefully prepared playhouse text, perhaps a prompt-book, and possibly prepared by the author's own hand. The rather elaborate stage directions seem to suggest the author's handiwork. Nevertheless, scholars do not all agree that the Folio text is a good one in view of the number of mislineations and verbal corruptions. Some have argued, however, that Shakespeare in this period wrote in a freer form and that the so-called mislineations are often deliberate.

The stage history of *Coriolanus* is obscure. We do not know where it was first produced or how it was received by Shakespeare's contemporaries. It has never been one of the popular plays, but through the centuries it has had occasional revivals. During the period of the Restoration, Nahum Tate made an adaptation which he produced in 1681–1682 at Drury Lane under the title of *The Ingratitude of a Commonwealth, or, The Fall of Caius Martius Coriolanus*. Tate tried to make his play a political tract for the times by identifying the demagogic tribunes with the Whig politicians of his own day. In 1719 John Dennis prepared another adaptation under the title of *The Invader of His Country, or, The Fatal Resentment*, which also had political overtones reflecting the Jacobite rebellion of 1715. In 1720 Shakespeare's *Coriolanus* unaltered was revived at Lincoln's Inn Fields, and it was again revived by Garrick at Drury Lane in 1754 to try to forestall a rival version at Covent Garden which combined elements from Shakespeare's play and from one written on the same theme by James Thomson which had been produced in 1749.

John Philip Kemble produced an adaptation of *Coriolanus* in 1789 with himself in the title role and Mrs. Siddons playing Volumnia. Edmund Kean revived Shakespeare's version in 1820 and played the title role at intervals. Throughout the nineteenth and first half of the twentieth centuries *Coriolanus* was acted at fairly frequent intervals. It has never been a wildly successful play, but it has stayed alive in the theatre. Late nineteenth-century and twentieth-century productions for the most part have eschewed earlier adaptations and stuck to Shakespeare's text. Although never a popular play in the study or on the stage, *Coriolanus* has retained a curious fascination for a public that has not been willing to let it die.

THE AUTHOR

As early as 1598 Shakespeare was so well known as a literary and dramatic craftsman that Francis Meres, in his *Palladis Tamia: Wits Treasury*, referred in flattering terms to him as "mellifluous and honey-tongued Shakespeare," famous for his *Venus and Adonis*, his *Lucrece*, and "his sugared sonnets," which were circulating "among his private friends." Meres observes further that "as Plautus and Seneca are accounted the best for comedy and tragedy among the Latins, so Shakespeare among the English is the most excellent in both kinds for the stage," and he mentions a dozen plays that had made a name for Shakespeare. He concludes with the remark "that the Muses would speak with Shakespeare's fine filed phrase if they would speak English."

To those acquainted with the history of the Elizabethan and Jacobean periods, it is incredible that anyone should be so naïve or ignorant as to doubt the reality of Shakespeare as the author of the plays that bear his name. Yet so much nonsense has been written about other "candidates" for the plays that it is well to remind readers that no credible evidence that would stand up in a court of law has ever been adduced to prove either that Shakespeare did not write his plays or that anyone else wrote

The Droeshout engraving of William Shakespeare.
From the title page of the First Folio

them. All the theories offered for the authorship of Francis Bacon, the Earl of Derby, the Earl of Oxford, the Earl of Hertford, Christopher Marlowe, and a score of other candidates are mere conjectures spun from the active imaginations of persons who confuse hypothesis and conjecture with evidence.

As Meres' statement of 1598 indicates, Shakespeare was already a popular playwright whose name carried weight at the box office. The obvious reputation of Shakespeare as early as 1598 makes the effort to prove him a myth one of the most absurd in the history of human perversity.

The anti-Shakespeareans talk darkly about a plot of vested interests to maintain the authorship of Shakespeare. Nobody has any vested interest in Shakespeare, but every scholar is interested in the truth and in the quality of evidence advanced by special pleaders who set forth hypotheses in place of facts.

The anti-Shakespeareans base their arguments upon a few simple premises, all of them false. These false premises are that Shakespeare was an unlettered yokel without any schooling, that nothing is known about Shakespeare, and that only a noble lord or the equivalent in background could have written the plays. The facts are that more is known about Shakespeare than about most dramatists of his day, that he had a very good education, acquired in the Stratford Grammar School, that the plays show no evidence of profound book learning, and that the knowledge of kings and courts evident in the plays is no greater than any intelligent young man could have picked up at second hand. Most anti-Shakespeareans are naïve and betray an obvious snobbery. The author of their favorite plays, they imply, must have had a college diploma framed and hung on his study wall like the one in their dentist's office, and obviously so great a writer must have had a title or some equally significant evidence of exalted social background. They forget that genius has a way of cropping up in unexpected places and that none of the great creative writers of the world got his inspiration in a college or university course.

William Shakespeare was the son of John Shakespeare of Stratford-upon-Avon, a substantial citizen of that small but busy market town in the center of the rich agricultural county of Warwick. John Shakespeare kept a shop, what we would call a general store; he dealt in wool and other produce and gradually acquired property. As a youth, John Shakespeare had learned the trade of glover and leather worker. There is no contemporary evidence that the elder Shakespeare was a butcher, though the anti-Shakespeareans like to talk about the ignorant "butcher's boy of Stratford." Their only evidence is a statement by gossipy John Aubrey, more than a century after William Shakespeare's birth, that young William followed his father's trade, and when he killed a calf, "he would do it in a high style and make a speech." We would like to believe the story true, but Aubrey is not a very credible witness.

John Shakespeare probably continued to operate a farm at Snitterfield that his father had leased. He married Mary Arden, daughter of his father's landlord, a man of some property. The third of their eight children was William, baptized on April 26, 1564, and probably born three days before. At least, it is conventional to celebrate April 23 as his birthday.

The Stratford records give considerable information about John Shakespeare. We know that he held several municipal offices including those of alderman and mayor. In 1580 he was in some sort of legal difficulty and was fined for neglecting a summons of the Court of Queen's Bench requiring him to appear at Westminster and be bound over to keep the peace.

As a citizen and alderman of Stratford, John Shakespeare was entitled to send his son to the grammar school free. Though the records are lost, there can be no reason to doubt that this is where young William received his education. As any student of the period knows, the grammar schools provided the basic education in Latin learning and literature. The Elizabethan grammar school is not to be confused with modern grammar schools. Many cultivated men of the day received all their formal education in the grammar schools. At the universities in this period a student would have received little training that would have inspired him to be a creative writer. At Stratford young Shakespeare would have acquired a familiarity with Latin and some little knowledge of Greek. He would have read Latin authors and become acquainted with the plays of Plautus and Terence. Undoubtedly, in this period of his life he received that stimulation to read and explore for himself the world of ancient and modern history which he later utilized in his plays. The youngster who does not acquire this type of intellectual curiosity *before* college days rarely develops as a result of a college course the kind of mind Shakespeare demonstrated. His learning in books was anything but profound, but he clearly had the probing curiosity that sent him in search of information, and he had a keenness in the observation of nature and of humankind that finds reflection in his poetry.

There is little documentation for Shakespeare's boyhood. There is little reason why there should be. Nobody knew that he was going to be a dramatist about whom any scrap of information would be prized in the centuries to come. He was merely an active and vigorous youth of Stratford, perhaps assisting his father in his business, and no Boswell bothered to write down facts about him. The most important record that we have is a marriage license issued by the Bishop of Worcester on November 28, 1582, to permit William Shakespeare to marry Anne Hathaway, seven or eight years his senior; furthermore, the Bishop permitted the marriage after reading the banns only once instead of three times, evidence of the desire for haste. The need was explained on May 26, 1583, when the christening of Susanna, daughter of William and Anne Shakespeare, was recorded at Stratford. Two years later, on February 2, 1585, the records show the birth of twins to the Shakespeares, a boy and a girl who were christened Hamnet and Judith.

What William Shakespeare was doing in Stratford during the early years of his married life, or when he went to London, we do not know. It has been conjectured that he tried his hand at schoolteaching, but that is a mere guess. There is a legend that he left Stratford to escape a charge of poaching in the park of Sir Thomas Lucy of Charlecote, but there is no proof of this. There is also a legend that when first he came to London, he earned his living by holding horses outside a playhouse and presently was given employment inside, but there is nothing better than eighteenth-century hearsay for this. How Shakespeare broke into the London theatres as a dramatist and actor we do not know. But lack of information is not surprising, for Elizabethans did not write their autobiographies, and we know even less about the lives of many writers and some men of affairs than we know about Shakespeare. By 1592 he was so well established and popular that he incurred the envy of the dramatist and pamphleteer Robert Greene, who referred to him as an "upstart crow . . . in his own conceit the only Shake-scene in a country." From this time onward, contemporary allusions and references in legal documents enable the scholar to chart Shakespeare's career with greater accuracy than is possible with most other Elizabethan dramatists.

By 1594 Shakespeare was a member of the com-

Shakespear if Player
by Garter

Sketch of Shakespeare's coat of arms
From a sixteenth-century manuscript

pany of actors known as the Lord Chamberlain's
Men. After the accession of James I, in 1603, the
company would have the sovereign for their patron
and would be known as the King's Men. During the
period of its greatest prosperity, this company
would have as its principal theatres the Globe and
the Blackfriars. Shakespeare was both an actor and
a shareholder in the company. Tradition has assigned him such acting roles as Adam in *As You
Like It* and the Ghost in *Hamlet*, a modest place
on the stage that suggests that he may have had
other duties in the management of the company.
Such conclusions, however, are based on surmise.

What we do know is that his plays were popular
and that he was highly successful in his vocation.
His first play may have been *The Comedy of Er-
rors*, acted perhaps in 1591. Certainly this was one
of his earliest plays. The three parts of *Henry VI*
were acted sometime between 1590 and 1592.
Critics are not in agreement about precisely how
much Shakespeare wrote of these three plays.
Richard III probably dates from 1593. With this
play Shakespeare captured the imagination of Elizabethan audiences, then enormously interested in
historical plays. With *Richard III* Shakespeare also
gave an interpretation pleasing to the Tudors of the
rise to power of the grandfather of Queen Elizabeth.
From this time onward, Shakespeare's plays followed
on the stage in rapid succession: *Titus Andronicus,
The Taming of the Shrew, The Two Gentlemen of
Verona, Love's Labor's Lost, Romeo and Juliet, Richard II, A Midsummer Night's Dream, King John,*

The Merchant of Venice, Henry IV (Parts 1 and 2), Much Ado About Nothing, Henry V, Julius Cæsar, As You Like It, Twelfth Night, Hamlet, The Merry Wives of Windsor, All's Well That Ends Well, Measure for Measure, Othello, King Lear, and nine others that followed before Shakespeare retired completely, about 1613.

In the course of his career in London, he made enough money to enable him to retire to Stratford with a competence. His purchase on May 4, 1597, of New Place, then the second-largest dwelling in Stratford, a "pretty house of brick and timber," with a handsome garden, indicates his increasing prosperity. There his wife and children lived while he busied himself in the London theatres. The summer before he acquired New Place, his life was darkened by the death of his only son, Hamnet, a child of eleven. In May, 1602, Shakespeare purchased one hundred and seven acres of fertile farmland near Stratford and a few months later bought a cottage and garden across the alley from New Place. About 1611, he seems to have returned permanently to Stratford, for the next year a legal document refers to him as "William Shakespeare of Stratford-upon-Avon . . . gentleman." To achieve the desired appellation of gentleman, William Shakespeare had seen to it that the College of Heralds in 1596 granted his father a coat of arms. In one step he thus became a second-generation gentleman.

Shakespeare's daughter Susanna made a good match in 1607 with Dr. John Hall, a prominent and prosperous Stratford physician. His second daughter, Judith, did not marry until she was thirty-two years old, and then, under somewhat scandalous circumstances, she married Thomas Quiney, a Stratford vintner. On March 25, 1616, Shakespeare made his will, bequeathing his landed property to Susanna, £300 to Judith, certain sums to other relatives, and his second-best bed to his wife, Anne. Much has been made of the second-best bed, but the legacy probably indicates only that Anne liked that particular bed. Shakespeare, following the practice of the time, may have already arranged with Susanna for his wife's care. Finally, on April 23, 1616, the anniversary of his birth, William Shakespeare died, and he was buried on April 25 within the chancel of Trinity Church, as befitted an honored citizen. On August 6, 1623, a few months before the publication of the collected edition of Shakespeare's plays, Anne Shakespeare joined her husband in death.

THE PUBLICATION OF HIS PLAYS

During his lifetime Shakespeare made no effort to publish any of his plays, though eighteen appeared in print in single-play editions known as quartos. Some of these are corrupt versions known as "bad quartos." No quarto, so far as is known, had the author's approval. Plays were not considered "literature" any more than most radio and television scripts today are considered literature. Dramatists sold their plays outright to the theatrical companies and it was usually considered in the company's interest to keep plays from getting into print. To achieve a reputation as a man of letters, Shakespeare wrote his *Sonnets* and his narrative poems, *Venus and Adonis* and *The Rape of Lucrece,* but he probably never dreamed that his plays would establish his reputation as a literary genius. Only Ben Jonson, a man known for his colossal conceit, had the crust to call his plays *Works,* as he did when he published an edition in 1616. But men laughed at Ben Jonson.

After Shakespeare's death, two of his old colleagues in the King's Men, John Heminges and Henry Condell, decided that it would be a good thing to print, in more accurate versions than were then available, the plays already published and eighteen additional plays not previously published in quarto. In 1623 appeared *Mr. William Shakespeares Comedies, Histories, & Tragedies. Published according to the True Originall Copies. London. Printed by Isaac Iaggard and Ed. Blount.* This was the famous First Folio, a work that had the authority of Shakespeare's associates. The only play commonly attributed to Shakespeare that was omitted in the First Folio was *Pericles.* In their preface, "To the great Variety of Readers," Heminges and Condell state that whereas "you were abused with diverse stolen and surreptitious copies, maimed and deformed by the frauds and stealths of injurious impostors that exposed them, even those are now offered to your view cured and perfect of their limbs; and all the rest, absolute in their numbers, as he conceived them." What they used for print-er's copy is one of the vexed problems of scholarship, and skilled bibliographers have devoted years of study to the question of the relation of the "copy" for the First Folio to Shakespeare's manuscripts. In some cases it is clear that the editors corrected printed quarto versions of the plays, probably by comparison with playhouse scripts. Whether these scripts were in Shakespeare's autograph is anybody's guess. No manuscript of any play in Shakespeare's handwriting has survived. Indeed, very few play manuscripts from this period by any author are extant. The Tudor and Stuart periods had not yet learned to prize autographs and authors' original manuscripts.

Since the First Folio contains eighteen plays not previously printed, it is the only source for these. For the other eighteen, which had appeared in quarto versions, the First Folio also has the authority of an edition prepared and overseen by Shakespeare's colleagues and professional associates. But since editorial standards in 1623 were far from strict, and Heminges and Condell were actors rather than editors by profession, the texts are sometimes careless. The printing and proofreading of the First Folio also left much to be desired, and some garbled passages have had to be corrected and emended. The "good quarto" texts have to be taken into account in preparing a modern edition.

Because of the great popularity of Shakespeare through the centuries, the First Folio has become a prized book, but it is not a very rare one, for it is estimated that 238 copies are extant. The Folger

Shakespeare Library in Washington, D.C., has seventy-nine copies of the First Folio, collected by the founder, Henry Clay Folger, who believed that a collation of as many texts as possible would reveal significant facts about the text of Shakespeare's plays. Dr. Charlton Hinman, using an ingenious machine of his own invention for mechanical collating, has made many discoveries that throw light on Shakespeare's text and on printing practices of the day.

The probability is that the First Folio of 1623 had an edition of between 1,000 and 1,250 copies. It is believed that it sold for £1, which made it an expensive book, for £1 in 1623 was equivalent to something between $40 and $50 in modern purchasing power.

During the seventeenth century, Shakespeare was sufficiently popular to warrant three later editions in folio size, the Second Folio of 1632, the Third Folio of 1663–1664, and the Fourth Folio of 1685. The Third Folio added six other plays ascribed to Shakespeare, but these are apocryphal.

THE SHAKESPEAREAN THEATRE

The theatres in which Shakespeare's plays were performed were vastly different from those we know today. The stage was a platform that jutted out into the area now occupied by the first rows of seats on the main floor, what is called the "orchestra" in America and the "pit" in England. This platform had no curtain to come down at the ends of acts and scenes. And although simple stage properties were available, the Elizabethan theatre lacked both the machinery and the elaborate movable scenery of the modern theatre. In the rear of the platform stage was a curtained area that could be used as an inner room, a tomb, or any such scene that might be required. A balcony above this inner room, and perhaps balconies on the sides of the stage, could represent the upper deck of a ship, the entry to Juliet's room, or a prison window. A trap door in the stage provided an entrance for ghosts and devils from the nether regions, and a similar trap in the canopied structure over the stage, known as the "heavens," made it possible to let down angels on a rope. These primitive stage arrangements help to account for many elements in Elizabethan plays. For example, since there was no curtain, the dramatist frequently felt the necessity of writing into his play action to clear the stage at the ends of acts and scenes. The funeral march at the end of *Hamlet* is not there merely for atmosphere; Shakespeare had to get the corpses off the stage. The lack of scenery also freed the dramatist from undue concern about the exact location of his sets, and the physical relation of his various settings to each other did not have to be worked out with the same precision as in the modern theatre.

Before London had buildings designed exclusively for theatrical entertainment, plays were given in inns and taverns. The characteristic inn of the period had an inner courtyard with rooms opening onto balconies overlooking the yard. Players could set up

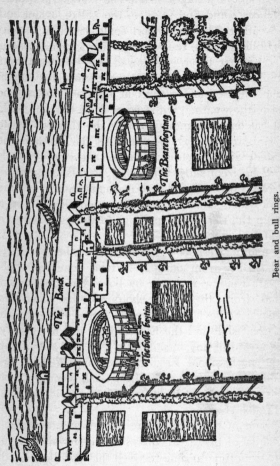

Bear and bull rings.

From Agas' *Map of London* (reproduced from J. Q. Adams, *Shakespearean Playhouses*).

their temporary stages at one end of the yard and audiences could find seats on the balconies out of the weather. The poorer sort could stand or sit on the cobblestones in the yard, which was open to the sky. The first theatres followed this construction, and throughout the Elizabethan period the large public theatres had a yard in front of the stage open to the weather, with two or three tiers of covered balconies extending around the theatre. This physical structure again influenced the writing of plays. Because a dramatist wanted the actors to be heard, he frequently wrote into his play orations that could be delivered with declamatory effect. He also provided spectacle, buffoonery, and broad jests to keep the riotous groundlings in the yard entertained and quiet.

In another respect the Elizabethan theatre differed greatly from ours. It had no actresses. All women's roles were taken by boys, sometimes recruited from the boys' choirs of the London churches. Some of these youths acted their roles with great skill and the Elizabethans did not seem to be aware of any incongruity. The first actresses on the professional English stage appeared after the Restoration of Charles II, in 1660, when exiled Englishmen brought back from France practices of the French stage.

London in the Elizabethan period, as now, was the center of theatrical interest, though wandering actors from time to time traveled through the country performing in inns, halls, and the houses of the nobility. The first professional playhouse, called

simply The Theatre, was erected by James Burbage, father of Shakespeare's colleague Richard
Burbage, in 1576 on lands of the old Holywell
Priory adjacent to Finsbury Fields, a playground
and park area just north of the city walls. It had the
advantage of being outside the city's jurisdiction
and yet was near enough to be easily accessible.
Soon after The Theatre was opened, another playhouse called The Curtain was erected in the same
neighborhood. Both of these playhouses had open
courtyards and were probably polygonal in shape.

About the time The Curtain opened, Richard
Farrant, Master of the Children of the Chapel
Royal at Windsor and of St. Paul's, conceived the
idea of opening a "private" theatre in the old monastery buildings of the Blackfriars, not far from St.
Paul's Cathedral in the heart of the city. This theatre was ostensibly to train the choirboys in plays
for presentation at Court, but Farrant managed to
present plays to paying audiences and achieved
considerable success until aristocratic neighbors
complained and had the theatre closed. This first
Blackfriars Theatre was significant, however, because it popularized the boy actors in a professional
way and it paved the way for a second theatre in
the Blackfriars, which Shakespeare's company took
over more than thirty years later. By the last years
of the sixteenth century, London had at least six
professional theatres and still others were erected
during the reign of James I.

The Globe Theatre, the playhouse that most people connect with Shakespeare, was erected early in

The Globe Playhouse.
From Visscher's *View of London* (1616).

1599 on the Bankside, the area across the Thames from the city. Its construction had a dramatic beginning, for on the night of December 28, 1598, James Burbage's sons, Cuthbert and Richard, gathered together a crew who tore down the old theatre in Holywell and carted the timbers across the river to a site that they had chosen for a new playhouse. The reason for this clandestine operation was a row with the landowner over the lease to the Holywell property. The site chosen for the Globe was another playground outside of the city's jurisdiction, a region of somewhat unsavory character. Not far away was the Bear Garden, an amphitheatre devoted to the baiting of bears and bulls. This was also the region occupied by many houses of ill fame licensed by the Bishop of Winchester and the source of substantial revenue to him. But it was easily accessible either from London Bridge or by means of the cheap boats operated by the London watermen, and it had the great advantage of being beyond the authority of the Puritanical aldermen of London, who frowned on plays because they lured apprentices from work, filled their heads with improper ideas, and generally exerted a bad influence. The aldermen also complained that the crowds drawn together in the theatre helped to spread the plague.

The Globe was the handsomest theatre up to its time. It was a large building, apparently octagonal in shape and open like its predecessors to the sky in the center, but capable of seating a large audience in its covered balconies. To erect and operate the Globe, the Burbages organized a syndicate composed of the leading members of the dramatic company, of which Shakespeare was a member. Since it was open to the weather and depended on natural light, plays had to be given in the afternoon. This caused no hardship in the long afternoons of an English summer, but in the winter the weather was a great handicap and discouraged all except the hardiest. For that reason, in 1608 Shakespeare's company was glad to take over the lease of the second Blackfriars Theatre, a substantial, roomy hall reconstructed within the framework of the old monastery building. This theatre was protected from the weather and its stage was artificially lighted by chandeliers of candles. This became the winter playhouse for Shakespeare's company and at once proved so popular that the congestion of traffic created an embarrassing problem. Stringent regulations had to be made for the movement of coaches in the vicinity. Shakespeare's company continued to use the Globe during the summer months. In 1613 a squib fired from a cannon during a performance of *Henry VIII* fell on the thatched roof and the Globe burned to the ground. The next year it was rebuilt.

London had other famous theatres. The Rose, just west of the Globe, was built by Philip Henslowe, a semiliterate denizen of the Bankside, who became one of the most important theatrical owners and producers of the Tudor and Stuart periods. What is more important for historians, he kept a detailed account book, which provides much of our informa-

Interior of the Swan Theatre.
From a drawing by Johannes de Witt (1596).

tion about theatrical history in his time. Another famous theatre on the Bankside was the Swan, which a Dutch priest, Johannes de Witt, visited in 1596. The crude drawing of the stage which he made was copied by his friend Arend van Buchell; it is one of the important pieces of contemporary evidence for theatrical construction. Among the other theatres, the Fortune, north of the city, on Golding Lane, and the Red Bull, even farther away from the city, off St. John's Street, were the most popular. The Red Bull, much frequented by apprentices, favored sensational and sometimes rowdy plays.

The actors who kept all of these theatres going were organized into companies under the protection of some noble patron. Traditionally actors had enjoyed a low reputation. In some of the ordinances they were classed as vagrants; in the phraseology of the time, "rogues, vagabonds, sturdy beggars, and common players" were all listed together as undesirables. To escape penalties often meted out to these characters, organized groups of actors managed to gain the protection of various personages of high degree. In the later years of Elizabeth's reign, a group flourished under the name of the Queen's Men; another group had the protection of the Lord Admiral and were known as the Lord Admiral's Men. Edward Alleyn, son-in-law of Philip Henslowe, was the leading spirit in the Lord Admiral's Men. Besides the adult companies, troupes of boy actors from time to time also enjoyed considerable popularity. Among these were the Children of Paul's and the Children of the Chapel Royal.

The company with which Shakespeare had a long association had for its first patron Henry Carey, Lord Hunsdon, the Lord Chamberlain, and hence they were known as the Lord Chamberlain's Men. After the accession of James I, they became the King's Men. This company was the great rival of the Lord Admiral's Men, managed by Henslowe and Alleyn.

All was not easy for the players in Shakespeare's time, for the aldermen of London were always eager for an excuse to close up the Blackfriars and any other theatres in their jurisdiction. The theatres outside the jurisdiction of London were not immune from interference, for they might be shut up by order of the Privy Council for meddling in politics or for various other offenses, or they might be closed in time of plague lest they spread infection. During plague times, the actors usually went on tour and played the provinces wherever they could find an audience. Particularly frightening were the plagues of 1592–1594 and 1613 when the theatres closed and the players, like many other Londoners, had to take to the country.

Though players had a low social status, they enjoyed great popularity, and one of the favorite forms of entertainment at court was the performance of plays. To be commanded to perform at court conferred great prestige upon a company of players, and printers frequently noted that fact when they published plays. Several of Shakespeare's plays were performed before the sovereign, and Shakespeare himself undoubtedly acted in some of these plays.

REFERENCES FOR FURTHER READING

Many readers will want suggestions for further reading about Shakespeare and his times. The literature in this field is enormous but a few references will serve as guides to further study. A simple and useful little book is Gerald Sanders, *A Shakespeare Primer* (New York, 1950). *A Companion to Shakespeare Studies,* edited by Harley Granville-Barker and G. B. Harrison (Cambridge, Eng., 1934) is a valuable guide. More detailed but still not so voluminous as to be confusing is Hazelton Spencer, *The Art and Life of William Shakespeare* (New York, 1940) which, like Sanders' handbook, contains a brief annotated list of useful books on various aspects of the subject. The most detailed and scholarly work providing complete factual information about Shakespeare is Sir Edmund Chambers, *William Shakespeare: A Study of Facts and Problems* (2 vols., Oxford, 1930). For detailed, factual information about the Elizabethan and seventeenth-century stages, the definitive reference works are Sir Edmund Chambers, *The Elizabethan Stage* (4 vols., Oxford, 1923) and Gerald E. Bentley, *The Jacobean and Caroline Stage* (5 vols., Oxford, 1941–1956). Alfred Harbage, *Shakespeare's Audience* (New York, 1941) and Martin Holmes,

Shakespeare's Public (London, 1960) throw light on the nature and tastes of the customers for whom Elizabethan dramatists wrote.

Although specialists disagree about details of stage construction, the reader will find essential information in John C. Adams, *The Globe Playhouse: Its Design and Equipment* (Barnes & Noble, 1961). An excellent description of the architecture of the Globe is Irwin Smith, *Shakespeare's Globe Playhouse: A Modern Reconstruction in Text and Scale Drawings Based upon the Reconstruction of the Globe by John Cranford Adams* (New York, 1956). Another recent study of the physical characteristics of the Globe is C. Walter Hodges, *The Globe Restored* (London, 1953). A. M. Nagler's *Shakespeare's Stage* (New Haven, 1958) presents a lucid synthesis of available information on the physical conditions in theatres of Shakespeare's age.

The following titles on theatrical history will provide information about Shakespeare's plays in later periods: Alfred Harbage, *Theatre for Shakespeare* (Toronto, 1955); Esther Cloudman Dunn, *Shakespeare in America* (New York, 1939); George C. D. Odell, *Shakespeare from Betterton to Irving* (2 vols., London, 1921); Arthur Colby Sprague, *Shakespeare and the Actors: The Stage Business in His Plays (1660–1905)* (Cambridge, Mass., 1944) and *Shakespearian Players and Performances* (Cambridge, Mass., 1953); Leslie Hotson, *The Commonwealth and Restoration Stage* (Cambridge, Mass.,

1928); Alwin Thaler, *Shakspere to Sheridan: A Book About the Theatre of Yesterday and To-day* (Cambridge, Mass., 1922); Ernest Bradlee Watson, *Sheridan to Robertson: A Study of the 19th-Century London Stage* (Cambridge, Mass., 1926). Enid Welsford, *The Court Masque* (Cambridge, Mass., 1927) is an excellent study of the characteristics of this form of entertainment.

The question of the authenticity of Shakespeare's plays arouses perennial attention. A book that demolishes the notion of hidden cryptograms in the plays is William F. Friedman and Elizebeth S. Friedman, *The Shakespearean Ciphers Examined* (New York, 1957). A succinct account of the various absurdities advanced to suggest the authorship of a multitude of candidates other than Shakespeare will be found in R. C. Churchill, *Shakespeare and His Betters* (Bloomington, Ind., 1959) and Frank W. Wadsworth, *The Poacher from Stratford: A Partial Account of the Controversy over the Authorship of Shakespeare's Plays* (Berkeley, Calif., 1958). An essay on the curious notions in the writings of the anti-Shakespeareans is that by Louis B. Wright, "The Anti-Shakespeare Industry and the Growth of Cults," *The Virginia Quarterly Review*, XXXV (1959), 280-303.

Harley Granville-Barker, *Prefaces to Shakespeare* (5 vols., London, 1927–1948) provides stimulating critical discussion of the plays. An older classic of criticism is Andrew C. Bradley, *Shakespearean Tragedy: Lectures on Hamlet, Othello, King Lear,*

Macbeth (London, 1904), which is available in an inexpensive reprint (Now York, 1955). Thomas M. Parrott, *Shakespearean Comedy* (New York, 1949) is scholarly and readable. Shakespeare's dramatizations of English history are examined in E. M. W. Tillyard, *Shakespeare's History Plays* (London, 1948), and Lily Bess Campbell, *Shakespeare's "Histories," Mirrors of Elizabethan Policy* (San Marino, Calif., 1947), contains a more technical discussion of the same subject.

Reprints of some of the sources for Shakespeare's plays can be found in *Shakespeare's Library* (2 vols., 1850), edited by John Payne Collier, and *The Shakespeare Classics* (12 vols., 1907–1926), edited by Israel Gollancz. Geoffrey Bullough is the editor of a new series of volumes reprinting the sources, three volumes of which are in print covering the comedies and the early history plays (New York, 1957–). For discussion of Shakespeare's use of his sources see Kenneth Muir, *Shakespeare's Sources: Comedies and Tragedies* (London, 1957). Thomas M. Cranfill has edited a facsimile reprint of *Riche His Farewell to Military Profession* (1581), which contains stories which Shakespeare probably used for several of his plays.

Useful for the background of the theme of honor is Curtis B. Watson, *Shakespeare and the Renaissance Concept of Honor* (Princeton, N. J., 1960). Brents Stirling, *The Populace in Shakespeare* (New York, 1949), discusses the interpretation to be placed on Shakespeare's mob scenes in *Coriolanus* and in other plays. M. W. MacCallum, *Shakespeare's Roman Plays and Their Background* (London, 1910), provides a useful analysis of Shakespeare's use of his source. See also Hermann Heuer, "From Plutarch to Shakespeare: A Study of *Coriolanus*," *Shakespeare Survey*, X (1957), 50–59. Still provocative is A. C. Bradley, "Coriolanus," in the *Proceedings of the British Academy, 1911–1912* (London, 1912), Concise and sensible are the notes and discussion of this play by John Munro in *The London Shakespeare* (New York, 1958), vol. VI. Another useful edition is *The Tragedy of Coriolanus*, ed. by W. J. Craig and R. H. Case, The Arden Shakespeare (London, 1922).

Interesting pictures as well as new information about Shakespeare will be found in F. E. Halliday, *Shakespeare, a Pictorial Biography* (London, 1956). Allardyce Nicoll, *The Elizabethans* (Cambridge, Eng., 1957) contains a variety of illustrations for the period.

A brief, clear, and accurate account of Tudor history is S. T. Bindoff, *The Tudors,* in the Penguin series. A readable general history is G. M. Trevelyan, *The History of England,* first published in 1926 and available in many editions. G. M. Trevelyan, *English Social History,* first published in 1942 and also available in many editions, provides fascinating information about England in all periods. Sir John Neale, *Queen Elizabeth* (London, 1934) is the best study of the great Queen. Various aspects of life in the Elizabethan period are treated in Louis B. Wright, *Middle-Class Culture in Eliza-bethan England* (Chapel Hill, N. C., 1935: re-printed, Ithaca, N. Y., 1958). *Shakespeare's Eng-land: An Account of the Life and Manners of His Age,* ed. by Sidney Lee and C. T. Onions (2 vols., Oxford, 1916) provides a large amount of informa-tion on many aspects of life in the Elizabethan pe-riod. Additional information will be found in Muriel St. C. Byrne, *Elizabethan Life in Town and Coun-try* (Barnes & Noble, 1961).

The Folger Shakespeare Library is currently pub-lishing a series of illustrated pamphlets on various aspects of English life in the sixteenth and seven-teenth centuries. The following titles are available: Dorothy E. Mason, *Music in Elizabethan England;* Craig R. Thompson, *The English Church in the Sixteenth Century;* Louis B. Wright, *Shakespeare's Theatre and the Dramatic Tradition;* Giles E. Daw-son, *The Life of William Shakespeare;* Virginia A. LaMar, *English Dress in the Age of Shakespeare;* Craig R. Thompson, *The Bible in English, 1525–1611;* Craig R. Thompson, *Schools in Tudor Eng-land;* Craig R. Thompson, *Universities in Tudor England;* Lilly C. Stone, *English Sports and Rec-reations;* Conyers Read, *The Government of Eng-land under Elizabeth;* Virginia A. LaMar, *Travel and Roads in England;* John R. Hale, *The Art of War and Renaissance England;* and Albert J. Schmidt, *The Tudor and Stuart Yeoman.*

[Dramatis Personae

Caius Marcius, afterward *Caius Marcius Coriolanus*.

Titus Lartius,
Cominius, } generals against the Volscians.

Menenius Agrippa, friend to *Coriolanus.*

Sicinius Velutus,
Junius Brutus, } tribunes of the people.

Young Marcius, son to *Coriolanus.*

A Roman Herald.

Tullus Aufidius, general of the Volscians.

Lieutenant to *Aufidius.*

Conspirators with *Aufidius.*

Nicanor, a Roman in the service of the Volscians.

Adrian, a Volscian.

A citizen of Antium.

Two Volscian guards.

Volumnia, mother to *Coriolanus.*

Virgilia, wife to *Coriolanus.*

Valeria, friend to *Virgilia.*

Gentlewoman attending on *Virgilia.*

Roman and Volscian Senators, Patricians, Ædiles, Lictors, Soldiers, Citizens, Messengers, Servants to Aufidius, and other Attendants.

SCENE: Rome and the neighborhood; Corioli and the neighborhood; Antium.]

THE TRAGEDY OF

CORIOLANUS

ACT I

I. Caius Marcius, a Roman patrician, has earned great honor for his military prowess but is hated by the populace for his pride and the contempt he shows for the common people. They blame him in particular because in time of famine they have been denied corn at a low rate.

When word comes that the Volsces are preparing to attack Rome, however, Marcius is assigned a major role in meeting the enemy. Before the town of Corioli he displays great courage and rallies the faltering Romans until the city is taken. He receives full credit for the victory. The Roman general, Cominius, bestows upon him the title "Coriolanus" in honor of his actions at Corioli.

▬▬▬▬▬▬▬▬▬▬▬▬▬▬▬▬▬▬

I. i. 12. on't: of it.
18. guess: think.

ACT I

Scene I. [Rome. A street.]

Enter a company of mutinous Citizens, with staves,
clubs, and other weapons.

1. Cit. Before we proceed any further, hear me
speak.

All. Speak, speak.

1. Cit. You are all resolved rather to die than to
famish?   5

All. Resolved, resolved.

1. Cit. First, you know Caius Marcius is chief
enemy to the people.

All. We know't, we know't.

1. Cit. Let us kill him, and we'll have corn at our   10
own price. Is't a verdict?

All. No more talking on't; let it be done. Away,
away!

2. Cit. One word, good citizens.

1. Cit. We are accounted poor citizens, the patri-   15
cians good. What authority surfeits on would relieve
us; if they would yield us but the superfluity while it
were wholesome, we might guess they relieved us hu-

1

19. **they think we are too dear:** i.e., they consider such a course too great a price to pay for our good will.

20. **object:** spectacle.

21-2. **sufferance:** suffering.

23. **rakes:** that is, emaciated, referring to the proverbial saying "As lean as a rake."

27. **dog:** hound; persecutor.

38-9. **proud . . . to the altitude of his virtue:** i.e., his pride is as great as his reputation for virtue.

manely; but they think we are too dear. The leanness
that afflicts us, the object of our misery, is as an in-   20
ventory to particularize their abundance; our sufferance is a gain to them. Let us revenge this with our
pikes ere we become rakes; for the gods know I speak
this in hunger for bread, not in thirst for revenge.

2. Cit. Would you proceed especially against Caius   25
Marcius?

1. Cit. Against him first; he's a very dog to the com-
monalty.

2. Cit. Consider you what services he has done for
his country?   30

1. Cit. Very well, and could be content to give him
good report for't but that he pays himself with being
proud.

2. Cit. Nay, but speak not maliciously.

1. Cit. I say unto you, what he hath done famously   35
he did it to that end; though soft-conscienced men
can be content to say it was for his country, he did it
to please his mother and to be partly proud, which he
is, even to the altitude of his virtue.

2. Cit. What he cannot help in his nature you ac-   40
count a vice in him. You must in no way say he is
covetous.

1. Cit. If I must not, I need not be barren of accusations; he hath faults, with surplus, to tire in repetition.   *Shouts within.* 45
What shouts are these? The other side o' the city is
risen. Why stay we prating here? To the Capitol!

All. Come, come.

1. Cit. Soft! Who comes here?

Enter Menenius Agrippa.

2. Cit. Worthy Menenius Agrippa; one that hath   50
always loved the people.

1. Cit. He's one honest enough; would all the rest
were so!

Men. What work's, my countrymen, in hand?
     Where go you   55
With bats and clubs? The matter? Speak, I pray you.

1. Cit. Our business is not unknown to the Senate;
they have had inkling this fortnight what we intend
to do, which now we'll show 'em in deeds. They say
poor suitors have strong breaths; they shall know we   60
have strong arms too.

Men. Why, masters, my good friends, mine honest
     neighbors,
Will you undo yourselves?

1. Cit. We cannot, sir; we are undone already.   65

Men. I tell you, friends, most charitable care
Have the patricians of you. For your wants,
Your suffering in this dearth, you may as well
Strike at the heaven with your staves as lift them
Against the Roman state, whose course will on   70
The way it takes, cracking ten thousand curbs
Of more strong link asunder than can ever
Appear in your impediment. For the dearth,
The gods, not the patricians, make it, and
Your knees to them, not arms, must help. Alack,   75
You are transported by calamity
Thither where more attends you; and you slander

78. **helms:** helmsmen; pilots.

93. **stale't:** Lewis Theobald's emendation of the Folio reading "scale't." The meaning is "give it further repetition."

95. **fob off our disgrace:** convince us that we have suffered no wrong.

100. **gulf:** voracious appetite.

106. **affection:** inclination.

The helms o' the state, who care for you like fathers,
When you curse them as enemies.

1. Cit. Care for us! True, indeed! They ne'er cared   80
for us yet. Suffer us to famish, and their storehouses
crammed with grain; make edicts for usury, to support usurers; repeal daily any wholesome act established against the rich, and provide more piercing
statutes daily to chain up and restrain the poor. If the   85
wars eat us not up, they will; and there's all the love
they bear us.

Men. Either you must
Confess yourselves wondrous malicious,
Or be accused of folly. I shall tell you   90
A pretty tale. It may be you have heard it;
But, since it serves my purpose, I will venture
To stale't a little more.

1. Cit. Well, I'll hear it, sir; yet you must not think
to fob off our disgrace with a tale. But, an't please   95
you, deliver.

Men. There was a time when all the body's mem-
    bers
Rebelled against the belly; thus accused it:
That only like a gulf it did remain   100
I' the midst o' the body, idle and unactive,
Still cupboarding the viand, never bearing
Like labor with the rest; where the other instruments
Did see and hear, devise, instruct, walk, feel,
And, mutually participate, did minister   105
Unto the appetite and affection common
Of the whole body. The belly answered—

1. Cit. Well, sir, what answer made the belly?

115. **for that:** because.
121. **muniments:** defenses.
125. **cormorant:** insatiable.
132. **you'st:** thou shalt.

Men. Sir, I shall tell you. With a kind of smile,
Which ne'er came from the lungs, but even thus—   110
For look you, I may make the belly smile
As well as speak—it tauntingly replied
To the discontented members, the mutinous parts
That envied his receipt; even so most fitly
As you malign our senators for that   115
They are not such as you.

1. Cit.   Your belly's answer—What?
The kingly crowned head, the vigilant eye,
The counselor heart, the arm our soldier,
Our steed the leg, the tongue our trumpeter,   120
With other muniments and petty helps
In this our fabric, if that they—

Men.   What then?
Fore me, this fellow speaks.. What then? What then?

1. Cit. Should by the cormorant belly be restrained,   125
Who is the sink o' the body—

Men.   Well, what then?

1. Cit. The former agents, if they did complain,
What could the belly answer?

Men.   I will tell you;   130
If you'll bestow a small—of what you have little—
Patience awhile, you'st hear the belly's answer.

1. Cit. Y'are long about it.

Men.   Note me this, good friend:
Your most grave belly was deliberate,   135
Not rash like his accusers, and thus answered.
"True is it, my incorporate friends," quoth he,
"That I receive the general food at first
Which you do live upon; and fit it is,

144. **cranks and offices:** winding passages and organs.

146. **competency:** sufficiency.

147. **though that:** though.

158. **digest:** think over and stomach.

168. **rascal, that art worst in blood to run:** hunting terminology. A **rascal** is an inferior specimen of a deer. **In blood** refers to the animal's physical condition. Menenius means that the citizen is such a poor specimen that he needs a head start.

Because I am the storehouse and the shop   140
Of the whole body. But, if you do remember,
I send it through the rivers of your blood,
Even to the court, the heart, to the seat o' the brain;
And, through the cranks and offices of man,
The strongest nerves and small inferior veins   145
From me receive that natural competency
Whereby they live. And though that all at once
You, my good friends"—this says the belly; mark me—
   1. Cit. Ay, sir; well, well.
   Men.   "Though all at once cannot   150
See what I do deliver out to each,
Yet I can make my audit up, that all
From me do back receive the flour of all,
And leave me but the bran." What say you to't?
   1. Cit. It was an answer. How apply you this?   155
   Men. The senators of Rome are this good belly,
And you the mutinous members; for, examine
Their counsels and their cares, digest things rightly
Touching the weal o' the common, you shall find
No public benefit which you receive   160
But it proceeds or comes from them to you,
And no way from yourselves. What do you think,
You, the great toe of this assembly?
   1. Cit. I the great toe? Why the great toe?
   Men. For that, being one o' the lowest, basest,   165
    poorest,
Of this most wise rebellion, thou goest foremost.
Thou rascal, that art worst in blood to run,
Leadst first to win some vantage.
But make you ready your stiff bats and clubs.   170

172. **bale:** poison.
189. **that justice:** the justice that.
190. **affections:** tastes.

Rome and her rats are at the point of battle;
The one side must have bale.

Enter Caius Marcius.

                           Hail, noble Marcius!
  Mar. Thanks. What's the matter, you dissentious
    rogues   175
That, rubbing the poor itch of your opinion,
Make yourselves scabs?
  1. Cit.   We have ever your good word.
  Mar. He that will give good words to thee will
    flatter   180
Beneath abhorring. What would you have, you curs,
That like nor peace nor war? The one affrights you,
The other makes you proud. He that trusts to you,
Where he should find you lions, finds you hares;
Where foxes, geese; you are no surer, no,   185
Than is the coal of fire upon the ice
Or hailstone in the sun. Your virtue is
To make him worthy whose offense subdues him,
And curse that justice did it. Who deserves greatness
Deserves your hate; and your affections are   190
A sick man's appetite, who desires most that
Which would increase his evil. He that depends
Upon your favors swims with fins of lead,
And hews down oaks with rushes. Hang ye! Trust ye?
With every minute you do change a mind   195
And call him noble that was now your hate,
Him vile that was your garland. What's the matter
That in these several places of the city

214. **quarry:** heap of dead men.

215. **quartered:** the punishment of traitors was to hang, draw, and quarter them. Coriolanus thinks that the rebellious plebeians deserve this fate.

216. **pick:** pitch.

219. **passing:** exceedingly.

228-29. **answered:** satisfied.

A Roman patrician. From Cesare Vecellio, *De gli habiti antichi et moderni* (1590).

You cry against the noble Senate, who,
Under the gods, keep you in awe, which else   200
Would feed on one another? What's their seeking?
  Men. For corn at their own rates, whereof they say
The city is well stored.
  Mar.   Hang 'em! They say!
They'll sit by the fire and presume to know   205
What's done i' the Capitol, who's like to rise,
Who thrives and who declines; side factions, and give
    out
Conjectural marriages, making parties strong,
And feebling such as stand not in their liking   210
Below their cobbled shoes. They say there's grain
    enough!
Would the nobility lay aside their ruth
And let me use my sword, I'd make a quarry
With thousands of these quartered slaves, as high   215
As I could pick my lance.
  Men. Nay, these are almost thoroughly persuaded;
For though abundantly they lack discretion,
Yet are they passing cowardly. But, I beseech you,
What say the other troop?   220
  Mar.   They are dissolved. Hang 'em!
They said they were an-hungry; sighed forth prov-
    erbs—
That hunger broke stone walls, that dogs must eat,
That meat was made for mouths, that the gods sent   225
    not
Corn for the rich men only. With these shreds
They vented their complainings; which being an-
    swered,

235. **emulation:** i.e., triumph at their defeat of the nobility. An obsolete meaning of **emulation** is "jealous rivalry."

239. **'Sdeath:** God's death.

242. **Win upon power:** win virtual control of the government from sheer strength.

242-43. **themes/For insurrection's arguing:** reasons for rebellion.

249-50. **vent/Our musty superfluity:** rid ourselves of our excess population, who are stale from inactivity.

And a petition granted them—a strange one,   230
To break the heart of generosity
And make bold power look pale—they threw their
    caps
As they would hang them on the horns o' the moon,
Shouting their emulation.   235
    Men.   What is granted them?
    Mar. Five tribunes, to defend their vulgar wisdoms,
Of their own choice. One's Junius Brutus—
Sicinius Velutus, and I know not. 'Sdeath!
The rabble should have first unroofed the city   240
Ere so prevailed with me; it will in time
Win upon power and throw forth greater themes
For insurrection's arguing.
    Men.   This is strange.
    Mar. Go get you home, you fragments.   245

Enter a Messenger, hastily.

    Mess. Where's Caius Marcius?
    Mar.   Here. What's the matter?
    Mess. The news is, sir, the Volsces are in arms.
    Mar. I am glad on't; then we shall ha' means to vent
Our musty superfluity. See, our best elders.   250

*Enter Cominius, Titus Lartius, with other Senators;
Junius Brutus and Sicinius Velutus.*

    1. Sen. Marcius, 'tis true that you have lately told
    us:
The Volsces are in arms.

255. **put you to't:** put you on your mettle; give you much trouble.

Mar.   They have a leader,
Tullus Aufidius, that will put you to't.   255
I sin in envying his nobility;
And were I anything but what I am,
I would wish me only he.
　　Com.   You have fought together?
　　Mar. Were half to half the world by the ears, and 260
　　　he
Upon my party, I'd revolt, to make
Only my wars with him. He is a lion
That I am proud to hunt.
　　1. Sen.   Then, worthy Marcius,   265
Attend upon Cominius to these wars.
　　Com. It is your former promise.
　　Mar.   Sir, it is;
And I am constant. Titus Lartius, thou
Shalt see me once more strike at Tullus' face.   270
What, art thou stiff? Standst out?
　　Lar.   No, Caius Marcius;
I'll lean upon one crutch and fight with t'other
Ere stay behind this business.
　　Men.   O, true bred!   275
　　1. Sen. Your company to the Capitol; where, I
　　　know,
Our greatest friends attend us.
　　Lar. [*To Cominius*]   Lead you on.
[*To Marcius*] Follow Cominius; we must follow you;   280
Right worthy you priority.
　　Com.   Noble Marcius!
　　1. Sen. [*To the Citizens*] Hence to your homes; be
　　　gone.

294. **gird:** taunt.

298. **Too proud to be so valiant:** too proud of being so valiant.

302. **brook:** endure.

309. **censure:** i.e., common opinion. **Censure** originally had no connotation of disapproval.

Mar. Nay, let them follow. 285
The Volsces have much corn: take these rats thither
To gnaw their garners. Worshipful mutineers,
Your valor puts well forth; pray follow.

                             Citizens steal away.
               Exeunt all but Sicinius and Brutus.

Sic. Was ever man so proud as is this Marcius?
Bru. He has no equal. 290
Sic. When we were chosen tribunes for the people—
Bru. Marked you his lip and eyes?
Sic.   Nay, but his taunts!
Bru. Being moved, he will not spare to gird the
    gods. 295
Sic. Bemock the modest moon.
Bru. The present wars devour him! He is grown
Too proud to be so valiant.
Sic.   Such a nature,
Tickled with good success, disdains the shadow 300
Which he treads on at noon. But I do wonder
His insolence can brook to be commanded
Under Cominius.
Bru.   Fame, at the which he aims—
In whom already he is well graced—cannot 305
Better be held nor more attained than by
A place below the first; for what miscarries
Shall be the general's fault, though he perform
To the utmost of a man, and giddy censure
Will then cry out of Marcius, "O, if he 310
Had borne the business!"
Sic.   Besides, if things go well,

313-14. Opinion, that so sticks on Marcius, shall/Of his demerits rob Cominius: that is, the high reputation that Marcius has earned will result in his receiving the credit for Cominius' success. **Demerits** means "deserts."

322. singularity: this word refers to Marcius' personal attribute of overweening pride.

━━━━━━━━━━━━━━━━━━━━━━━━━━━━━━━━━━━━━

I.[ii.]5-7. What ever have been thought on in this state/That could be brought to bodily act ere Rome/Had circumvention: what things have we ever proposed to do that were performed before Rome forestalled us.

10. pressed: impressed; conscripted.

Opinion, that so sticks on Marcius, shall
Of his demerits rob Cominius.
   Bru.   Come.   315
Half all Cominius' honors are to Marcius,
Though Marcius earned them not; and all his faults
To Marcius shall be honors, though indeed
In aught he merit not.
   Sic.   Let's hence and hear   320
How the dispatch is made, and in what fashion,
More than his singularity, he goes
Upon this present action.
   Bru.   Let's along.
                                Exeunt.

[Scene II. Corioli. The Senate House.]

Enter Tullus Aufidius with Senators of Corioli.

   1. Sen. So, your opinion is, Aufidius,
That they of Rome are ent'red in our counsels
And know how we proceed.
   Auf.   Is it not yours?
What ever have been thought on in this state   5
That could be brought to bodily act ere Rome
Had circumvention? 'Tis not four days gone
Since I heard thence; these are the words—I think
I have the letter here; yes, here it is:
[*Reads*] "They have pressed a power, but it is not 10
    known
Whether for east or west. The dearth is great,
The people mutinous; and it is rumored,

34. **remove:** repulse of the enemy.
39. **parcels:** portions.

Cominius, Marcius, your old enemy,
Who is of Rome worse hated than of you,   15
And Titus Lartius, a most valiant Roman,
These three lead on this preparation
Whither 'tis bent. Most likely 'tis for you;
Consider of it."

  1. Sen.   Our army's in the field;   20
We never yet made doubt but Rome was ready
To answer us.

  Auf.   Nor did you think it folly
To keep your great pretenses veiled till when
They needs must show themselves; which in the   25
    hatching,
It seemed, appeared to Rome. By the discovery
We shall be short'ned in our aim, which was
To take in many towns ere almost Rome
Should know we were afoot.   30

  2. Sen.   Noble Aufidius,
Take your commission; hie you to your bands;
Let us alone to guard Corioli.
If they set down before's, for the remove
Bring up your army; but I think you'll find   35
Th' have not prepared for us.

  Auf.   O, doubt not that!
I speak from certainties. Nay, more,
Some parcels of their power are forth already,
And only hitherward. I leave your honors.   40
If we and Caius Marcius chance to meet,
'Tis sworn between us we shall ever strike
Till one can do no more.

  All.   The gods assist you!

I. [iii.] 10. such a person: that is, one who had such a noble appearance.

15. oak: a garland of oak leaves symbolizing the valorous actions he had performed.

Auf. And keep your honors safe!   45
1. Sen.   Farewell.
2. Sen.   Farewell.
All. Farewell.

                                   Exeunt.

[Scene III. Rome. Marcius' house.]

*Enter Volumnia and Virgilia, mother and wife to
Marcius; they set them down on two low stools and
sew.*

Vol. I pray you, daughter, sing, or express yourself
in a more comfortable sort. If my son were my husband, I should freelier rejoice in that absence wherein
he won honor than in the embracements of his bed
where he would show most love. When yet he was but   5
tender-bodied, and the only son of my womb; when
youth with comeliness plucked all gaze his way;
when, for a day of kings' entreaties, a mother should
not sell him an hour from her beholding; I, consider-
ing how honor would become such a person—that it   10
was no better than picturelike to hang by the wall, if
renown made it not stir—was pleased to let him seek
danger where he was to find fame. To a cruel war I
sent him, from whence he returned his brows bound
with oak. I tell thee, daughter, I sprang not more in   15
joy at first hearing he was a man-child than now in
first seeing he had proved himself a man.

31. **shunning:** running from.

33. **got:** begot.

37. **Or:** either.

40. **trophy:** monument; i.e., blood is a more becoming ornament to a man than is gilding on his memorial; **Hecuba:** wife of King Priam of Troy.

42-3. **spit forth blood/At Grecian sword, contemning:** Hector is pictured as expressing his contempt for his Grecian adversary by the very vehemence with which his blood spurts from the wounds inflicted on him. The First Folio reads "contenning" which the Second Folio corrected to "contending." Contemning was suggested by early editors.

44. **fit:** ready.

45. **fell:** savage; deadly.

Vir. But had he died in the business, madam, how
then?

Vol. Then his good report should have been my   20
son; I therein would have found issue. Hear me pro-
fess sincerely: had I a dozen sons, each in my love
alike, and none less dear than thine and my good
Marcius, I had rather had eleven die nobly for their
country than one voluptuously surfeit out of action.   25

Enter a Gentlewoman.

Gent. Madam, the Lady Valeria is come to visit you.
Vir. Beseech you give me leave to retire myself.
Vol. Indeed you shall not.
Methinks I hear hither your husband's drum;
See him pluck Aufidius down by the hair;   30
As children from a bear, the Volsces shunning him.
Methinks I see him stamp thus, and call thus:
"Come on, you cowards! You were got in fear,
Though you were born in Rome." His bloody brow
With his mailed hand then wiping, forth he goes,   35
Like to a harvestman that's tasked to mow
Or all or lose his hire.
Vir. His bloody brow? O Jupiter, no blood!
Vol. Away, you fool! It more becomes a man
Than gilt his trophy. The breasts of Hecuba,   40
When she did suckle Hector, looked not lovelier
Than Hector's forehead when it spit forth blood
At Grecian sword, contemning. Tell Valeria
We are fit to bid her welcome.   *Exit Gentlewoman.*
Vir. Heavens bless my lord from fell Aufidius!   45

52. **spot:** embroidery pattern or stitch.

59-60. **confirmed countenance:** resolute expression.

65. **mammocked it:** tore it to pieces.

66. **on's:** of his.

68. **crack:** rogue.

70. **huswife:** housewife.

A Roman matron. From Cesare Vecellio, *De gli habiti antichi et moderni* (1590).

Vol. He'll beat Aufidius' head below his knee
And tread upon his neck.

[Re-]enter Gentlewoman, with Valeria and an usher.

Val. My ladies both, good day to you.
Vol. Sweet madam!
Vir. I am glad to see your ladyship.   50
Val. How do you both? You are manifest house-
keepers. What are you sewing here? A fine spot, in
good faith. How does your little son?
Vir. I thank your ladyship; well, good madam.
Vol. He had rather see the swords and hear a drum   55
than look upon his schoolmaster.
Val. O' my word, the father's son! I'll swear 'tis a
very pretty boy. O' my troth, I looked upon him a
Wednesday half an hour together; has such a confirmed countenance! I saw him run after a gilded but-   60
terfly; and when he caught it he let it go again, and
after it again, and over and over he comes, and up
again, catched it again; or whether his fall enraged
him, or how 'twas, he did so set his teeth and tear it.
O, I warrant, how he mammocked it!   65
Vol. One on's father's moods.
Val. Indeed, la, 'tis a noble child.
Vir. A crack, madam.
Val. Come, lay aside your stitchery; I must have you
play the idle huswife with me this afternoon.   70
Vir. No, good madam; I will not out of doors.
Val. Not out of doors!
Vol. She shall, she shall.

77. **lies in:** awaits the birth of a child.
81. **want:** lack.
85. **sensible:** sensitive; capable of sensation.

Vir. Indeed, no, by your patience; I'll not over the
threshold till my lord return from the wars.   75

Val. Fie, you confine yourself most unreasonably;
come, you must go visit the good lady that lies in.

Vir. I will wish her speedy strength, and visit her
with my prayers; but I cannot go thither.

Vol. Why, I pray you?   80

Vir. 'Tis not to save labor, nor that I want love.

Val. You would be another Penelope; yet they say
all the yarn she spun in Ulysses' absence did but fill
Ithaca full of moths. Come, I would your cambric
were sensible as your finger, that you might leave   85
pricking it for pity. Come, you shall go with us.

Vir. No, good madam, pardon me; indeed I will not
forth.

Val. In truth, la, go with me; and I'll tell you excellent news of your husband.   90

Vir. O, good madam, there can be none yet.

Val. Verily, I do not jest with you; there came news
from him last night.

Vir. Indeed, madam?

Val. In earnest, it's true; I heard a senator speak it.   95
Thus it is: the Volsces have an army forth; against
whom Cominius the general is gone, with one part of
our Roman power. Your lord and Titus Lartius are set
down before their city Corioli; they nothing doubt
prevailing and to make it brief wars. This is true, on 100
mine honor; and so, I pray, go with us.

Vir. Give me excuse, good madam; I will obey you
in everything hereafter.

109. **at a word:** in a word; say no more about it, I am determined.

░░░░░░░░░░░░░░░░░░░░░░░░░░░░░░░░░░

I.[iv.] 1. **met:** engaged in battle.
6. **spoke:** fought.
14. **'larum:** alarum; trumpet signal for battle to begin.

Roman catapult. From Guillaume Du Choul, *Discours de la religion des anciens Romains* (1581).

18

Vol. Let her alone, lady; as she is now, she will but
disease our better mirth.   105

Val. In troth, I think she would. Fare you well,
then. Come, good sweet lady. Prithee, Virgilia, turn
thy solemnness out o' door and go along with us.

Vir. No, at a word, madam; indeed I must not. I
wish you much mirth.   110

Val. Well then, farewell.

                                              Exeunt.

[Scene IV. Before Corioli.]

*Enter Marcius, Titus Lartius, with drum and colors,
with Captains and Soldiers. To them a Messenger.*

Mar. Yonder comes news; a wager—they have met.
Lar. My horse to yours, no.
Mar.   'Tis done.
Lar.   Agreed.
Mar. Say, has our general met the enemy?   5
Mess. They lie in view, but have not spoke as yet.
Lar. So, the good horse is mine.
Mar.   I'll buy him of you.
Lar. No, I'll not sell nor give him; lend you him I
   will   10
For half a hundred years. Summon the town.
Mar. How far off lie these armies?
Mess.   Within this mile and half.
Mar. Then shall we hear their 'larum, and they ours.
Now, Mars, I prithee, make us quick in work,   15

17. **fielded:** engaged on the battlefield.

19. **nor a man that fears you less than he:** a roundabout way of saying that Aufidius has not the slightest fear of Marcius.

29. **cloven:** split. He means that the ordered ranks have been broken by the force of the Volsces' assault.

31. **instruction:** i.e., order to act.

34. **proof:** impenetrable; impervious to fear. **Proof** is the stoutest armor.

Siege tactics. From Guillaume Du Choul, *Discours de la religion des anciens Romains* (1581).

That we with smoking swords may march from hence
To help our fielded friends! Come, blow thy blast.

They sound a parley. Enter two Senators with others,
on the walls of Corioli.

Tullus Aufidius, is he within your walls?
  1. Sen. No, nor a man that fears you less than he:
That's lesser than a little. (*Drum afar off.*) Hark, our   20
    drums
Are bringing forth our youth. We'll break our walls
Rather than they shall pound us up; our gates,
Which yet seem shut, we have but pinned with
    rushes;   25
They'll open of themselves. (*Alarum far off.*) Hark
    you far off!
There is Aufidius. List what work he makes
Amongst your cloven army.
  Mar.   O, they are at it!   30
  Lar. Their noise be our instruction. Ladders, ho!

Enter the army of the Volsces.

  Mar. They fear us not, but issue forth their city.
Now put your shields before your hearts, and fight
With hearts more proof than shields. Advance, brave
    Titus.   35
They do disdain us much beyond our thoughts,
Which makes me sweat with wrath. Come on, my fel-
    lows.

S.D. after l. 40. Marcius advances to the front of the stage at the conclusion of the action.

41. **the contagion of the south:** the unwholesome damp borne by the south wind. Wind from the south was believed to carry moisture along with it and be productive of sickness.

49. **home:** with deadly force.

53. **followed:** the reading of the Second Folio; the Folio has "followes."

He that retires, I'll take him for a Volsce,
And he shall feel mine edge.   40

Alarum. The Romans are beat back to their trenches.
[Re-]enter Marcius, cursing.

  Mar. All the contagion of the south light on you,
You shames of Rome! You herd of— Boils and plagues
Plaster you o'er, that you may be abhorred
Farther than seen, and one infect another
Against the wind a mile! You souls of geese   45
That bear the shapes of men, how have you run
From slaves that apes would beat! Pluto and hell!
All hurt behind! Backs red, and faces pale
With flight and agued fear! Mend and charge home,
Or, by the fires of heaven, I'll leave the foe   50
And make my wars on you. Look to't. Come on;
If you'll stand fast we'll beat them to their wives,
As they us to our trenches followed.

Another alarum. [The Volsces fly,] and Marcius fol-
lows them to the gates.

So, now the gates are ope; now prove good seconds;
'Tis for the followers fortune widens them,   55
Not for the fliers. Mark me, and do the like.
                          [Marcius] enters the gates.
  1. Sol. Foolhardiness; not I.
  2. Sol.   Nor I.
                          [Marcius is shut in.]

60. **To the pot:** i.e., to destruction. The phrase is presumed to derive from the cutting up of vegetables for cooking.

68. **sensibly outdares his senseless sword:** that is, although he is capable of sensation and emotion, his courage is more unshakable than his unfeeling sword.

69. **Thou art left:** i.e., you stand alone, peerless.

72. **Cato's:** Theobald's correction of the Folio's "Calues." Plutarch confirms the correction.

79. **fetch him off:** rescue him; **make remain alike:** stay with him to share his fate.

Roman foot soldiers. From Guillaume Du Choul, *Discours de la religion des anciens Romains* (1581).

1. Sol. See, they have shut him in.
All. To the pot, I warrant him.   *Alarum continues.*   60

[Re-]*enter Titus Lartius.*

Lar. What is become of Marcius?
All.   Slain, sir, doubtless.
1. Sol. Following the fliers at the very heels,
With them he enters; who, upon the sudden,
Clapped to their gates. He is himself alone,   65
To answer all the city.
    Lar.   O noble fellow!
Who sensibly outdares his senseless sword,
And when it bows stands up. Thou art left, Marcius;
A carbuncle entire, as big as thou art,   70
Were not so rich a jewel. Thou wast a soldier
Even to Cato's wish, not fierce and terrible
Only in strokes, but with thy grim looks and
The thunderlike percussion of thy sounds
Thou madest thine enemies shake, as if the world   75
Were feverous and did tremble.

[Re-]*enter Marcius, bleeding, assaulted by the enemy.*

1. Sol.   Look, sir.
    Lar.   O, 'tis Marcius!
Let's fetch him off, or make remain alike.
                    They fight, and all enter the city.

I. [v.] 3. **murrain:** plague.

S.D. after l. 3. **trumpet:** trumpeter.

5. **drachma:** a Greek coin equivalent to six obols, or less than ten cents.

6. **Irons of a doit:** swords worth a doit (valued at one-fourth of an English farthing); **doublets:** jackets. The hangman gained possession of the clothing of executed criminals.

12. **make good:** secure; capture.

18. **praise:** appraise.

20. **physical:** beneficial, like the taking of physic (medicine).

[Scene V. Corioli. A street.]

Enter certain Romans, with spoils.

1. Rom. This will I carry to Rome.
2. Rom. And I this.
3. Rom. A murrain on't! I took this for silver.
                    Alarum continues still afar off.

Enter Marcius and Titus [Lartius] with a trumpet.

Mar. See here these movers that do prize their hours
At a cracked drachma! Cushions, leaden spoons,   5
Irons of a doit, doublets that hangmen would
Bury with those that wore them, these base slaves,
Ere yet the fight be done, pack up. Down with them!
                    Exeunt [pillagers].
And hark, what noise the general makes! To him!
There is the man of my soul's hate, Aufidius,   10
Piercing our Romans; then, valiant Titus, take
Convenient numbers to make good the city;
Whilst I, with those that have the spirit, will haste
To help Cominius.
Lar.   Worthy sir, thou bleedst;   15
Thy exercise hath been too violent
For a second course of fight.
Mar.   Sir, praise me not;
My work hath yet not warmed me. Fare you well;
The blood I drop is rather physical   20

I. [vi.] **6. By interims and conveying gusts:**
borne by intermittent gusts of wind.

9. fronts: foreheads; faces.

Than dangerous to me. To Aufidius thus
I will appear, and fight.

   Lar.   Now the fair goddess Fortune
Fall deep in love with thee, and her great charms
Misguide thy opposers' swords! Bold gentleman,   25
Prosperity be thy page!

   Mar.   Thy friend no less
Than those she placeth highest! So farewell.

   Lar. Thou worthiest Marcius!   [*Exit Marcius.*]
Go sound thy trumpet in the market place;   30
Call thither all the officers o' the town,
Where they shall know our mind. Away!

                                     Exeunt.

[Scene VI. Near the camp of Cominius.]

Enter Cominius, as it were in retire, with Soldiers.

   Com. Breathe you, my friends. Well fought; we are
     come off
Like Romans, neither foolish in our stands
Nor cowardly in retire. Believe me, sirs,
We shall be charged again. Whiles we have struck,   5
By interims and conveying gusts we have heard
The charges of our friends. The Roman gods
Lead their successes as we wish our own,
That both our powers, with smiling fronts encoun-
     t'ring,   10
May give you thankful sacrifice!

13. **issued:** come forth.
20. **briefly:** not long ago.
21. **confound:** expend; use up.
32. **tabor:** small drum.

Enter a Messenger.

                        Thy news?
  Mess. The citizens of Corioli have issued
And given to Lartius and to Marcius battle;
I saw our party to their trenches driven,   15
And then I came away.
  Com.   Though thou speakst truth,
Methinks thou speakst not well. How long is't since?
  Mess. Above an hour, my lord.
  Com. 'Tis not a mile; briefly we heard their drums.   20
How couldst thou in a mile confound an hour,
And bring thy news so late?
  Mess.   Spies of the Volsces
Held me in chase, that I was forced to wheel
Three or four miles about; else had I, sir,   25
Half an hour since brought my report.

Enter Marcius.

  Com.   Who's yonder
That does appear as he were flayed? O gods!
He has the stamp of Marcius, and I have
Beforetime seen him thus.   30
  Mar.   Come I too late?
  Com. The shepherd knows not thunder from a tabor
More than I know the sound of Marcius' tongue
From every meaner man.
  Mar.   Come I too late?   35
  Com. Ay, if you come not in the blood of others,
But mantled in your own.

38. **clip:** embrace.

65. **How lies their battle:** how are their forces deployed.

68. **vaward:** vanguard; advance position.

Mar.   O! let me clip ye
In arms as sound as when I wooed; in heart
As merry as when our nuptial day was done,   40
And tapers burned to bedward.
     Com.   Flower of warriors,
How is't with Titus Lartius?
     Mar. As with a man busied about decrees:
Condemning some to death and some to exile;   45
Ransoming him or pitying, threat'ning the other;
Holding Corioli in the name of Rome
Even like a fawning greyhound in the leash,
To let him slip at will.
     Com.   Where is that slave   50
Which told me they had beat you to your trenches?
Where is he? Call him hither.
     Mar.   Let him alone;
He did inform the truth. But for our gentlemen,
The common file—a plague! Tribunes for them!   55
The mouse ne'er shunned the cat as they did budge
From rascals worse than they.
     Com.   But how prevailed you?
     Mar. Will the time serve to tell? I do not think.
Where is the enemy? Are you lords o' the field?   60
If not, why cease you till you are so?
     Com.   Marcius,
We have at disadvantage fought, and did
Retire to win our purpose.
     Mar. How lies their battle? Know you on which side   65
They have placed their men of trust?
     Com.   As I guess, Marcius,
Their bands i' the vaward are the Antiates,

74. endure: remain.

77. advanced: raised.

A Roman legionary. From Guillaume Du Choul, *Discours de la religion des anciens Romains* (1581).

Of their best trust; o'er them Aufidius,
Their very heart of hope.   70
  Mar.   I do beseech you,
By all the battles wherein we have fought,
By the blood we have shed together, by the vows
We have made to endure friends, that you directly
Set me against Aufidius and his Antiates;   75
And that you not delay the present, but,
Filling the air with swords advanced and darts,
We prove this very hour.
  Com.   Though I could wish
You were conducted to a gentle bath   80
And balms applied to you, yet dare I never
Deny your asking: take your choice of those
That best can aid your action.
  Mar.   Those are they
That most are willing. If any such be here—   85
As it were sin to doubt—that love this painting
Wherein you see me smeared; if any fear
Lesser his person than an ill report;
If any think brave death outweighs bad life
And that his country's dearer than himself;   90
Let him alone, or so many so minded,
Wave thus to express his disposition,
And follow Marcius. *They all shout and wave their*
   swords, take him up in their arms and cast up
            their caps.

O, me alone! Make you a sword of me?
If these shows be not outward, which of you   95
But is four Volsces? None of you but is
Able to bear against the great Aufidius

101. As cause will be obeyed: as occasion requires.

105. Make good this ostentation: i.e., confirm the martial spirit you have displayed.

━━━━━━━━━━━━━━━━━━━━━━━━━

I.[vii.]1. ports: gates.

3. centuries: companies of a hundred men.

Trumpeters of the Roman army. From Guillaume Du Choul, *Discours de la religion des anciens Romains* (1581).

A shield as hard as his. A certain number,
Though thanks to all, must I select from all; the rest
Shall bear the business in some other fight,   100
As cause will be obeyed. Please you to march;
And four shall quickly draw out my command,
Which men are best inclined.
   Com.   March on, my fellows;
Make good this ostentation, and you shall   105
Divide in all with us.
                                  Exeunt.

[Scene VII. The gates of Corioli.]

*Titus Lartius, having set a guard upon Corioli, going
with drum and trumpet toward Cominius and Caius
Marcius, enters with a Lieutenant, other Soldiers,
and a Scout.*

   Lar. So, let the ports be guarded; keep your duties
As I have set them down. If I do send, dispatch
Those centuries to our aid; the rest will serve
For a short holding. If we lose the field
We cannot keep the town.   5
   Lieut.   Fear not our care, sir.
   Lar. Hence, and shut your gates upon's.
Our guider, come; to the Roman camp conduct us.
                                  Exeunt.

I. [viii.] 4. **Afric:** Africa.

5. **fame and envy:** envied fame. An example of hendiadys; **Fix thy foot:** i.e., take up the proper stance for hand-to-hand combat.

16. **bragged progeny:** boasted progenitors. Aufidius refers to the legendary founding of Rome by Æneas after the destruction of Troy; Hector was Troy's mightiest scourge of the Greeks.

18. **Officious:** presumptuous.

19. **In your condemned seconds:** i.e., by giving me support in violation of the rules of single combat.

[Scene VIII. A field of battle.]

Alarum, as in battle. Enter Marcius and Aufidius
at several doors.

Mar. I'll fight with none but thee, for I do hate thee
Worse than a promise-breaker.
Auf.   We hate alike:
Not Afric owns a serpent I abhor
More than thy fame and envy. Fix thy foot.   5
Mar. Let the first budger die the other's slave,
And the gods doom him after!
Auf.   If I fly, Marcius,
Halloa me like a hare.
Mar.   Within these three hours, Tullus,   10
Alone I fought in your Corioli walls,
And made what work I pleased. 'Tis not my blood
Wherein thou seest me masked. For thy revenge
Wrench up thy power to the highest.
Auf.   Wert thou the Hector   15
That was the whip of your bragged progeny,
Thou shouldst not scape me here.
    Here they fight, and certain Volsces come in the aid
    of Aufidius. Marcius fights till they be driven in
                                              breathless.
Officious, and not valiant, you have shamed me
In your condemned seconds.
                                      Exeunt.

I. [**ix.**] Ent. **Flourish:** a triumphant series of notes on the trumpet; **retreat:** a trumpet signal for retreat.

2. **Thou't:** thou wouldst.

8. **fusty:** stale-smelling.

9. **against their hearts:** reluctantly.

11-2. **Yet camest thou to a morsel of this feast,/Having fully dined before:** i.e., your present deeds in comparison with the exploits you had already accomplished are as a morsel to a feast.

14. **Here is the steed, we the caparison:** i.e., Marcius is the agent of victory, we are only accessories. A **caparison** is the trapping of a horse.

17. **charter:** license; right; **blood:** blood kin; family.

[Scene IX. The Roman camp.]

Flourish. Alarum. A retreat is sounded. Enter, at one door, Cominius with the Romans; at another door, Marcius, with his arm in a scarf.

Com. If I should tell thee o'er this thy day's work,
Thou't not believe thy deeds; but I'll report it
Where senators shall mingle tears with smiles;
Where great patricians shall attend and shrug,
I' the end admire; where ladies shall be frighted   5
And, gladly quaked, hear more; where the dull tribunes,
That with the fusty plebeians hate thine honors,
Shall say against their hearts, "We thank the gods
Our Rome hath such a soldier."   10
Yet camest thou to a morsel of this feast,
Having fully dined before.

Enter Titus [Lartius,] with his power, from the pursuit.

Lar.   O General,
Here is the steed, we the caparison.
Hadst thou beheld—   15
    Mar.   Pray now, no more; my mother,
Who has a charter to extol her blood,
When she does praise me grieves me. I have done
As you have done—that's what I can; induced
As you have been—that's for my country.   20

21-2. He that has but effected his good will/ Hath overta'en mine act: anyone who has done his honest duty has equaled what I have done.

23-4. You shall not be/The grave of your deserving: you shall not bury your own merit.

36. tent themselves with death: infect rather than cure themselves. A **tent** is a probe used to cleanse a wound.

40-1 at/Your only choice: as you alone choose.

He that has but effected his good will
Hath overta'en mine act.

Com.   You shall not be
The grave of your deserving; Rome must know
The value of her own. 'Twere a concealment   25
Worse than a theft, no less than a traducement,
To hide your doings and to silence that
Which to the spire and top of praises vouched
Would seem but modest. Therefore, I beseech you,
In sign of what you are, not to reward   30
What you have done, before our army hear me.

Mar. I have some wounds upon me, and they smart
To hear themselves rememb'red.

Com.   ·   Should they not,
Well might they fester 'gainst ingratitude   35
And tent themselves with death. Of all the horses—
Whereof we have ta'en good, and good store—of all
The treasure in this field achieved and city,
We render you the tenth; to be ta'en forth
Before the common distribution at   40
Your only choice.

Mar.   I thank you, General,
But cannot make my heart consent to take
A bribe to pay my sword. I do refuse it,
And stand upon my common part with those   45
That have beheld the doing.

*A long flourish. They all cry "Marcius, Marcius!"
cast up their caps and lances. Cominius and Lartius stand bare.*

May these same instruments which you profane
Never sound more! When drums and trumpets shall

50. **soothing:** flattering; **steel:** armor.

52. **overture:** offer; i.e., let's enlist parasites to fight our battles. The meaning of this passage has been the subject of a great deal of discussion and one editor conjectured that the word should be changed to "coverture."

54. **foiled some debile wretch:** overcome some weak wretch. The phrase does not make clear the meaning "because I *have* foiled . . . wretch"; **note:** acclaim.

56. **hyperbolical:** extravagant; exaggerated.

57. **dieted:** fed; feasted.

61. **give:** describe.

63. **his proper harm:** harm to himself. **Proper** means "personal."

66. **garland:** trophy of victory.

72. **addition:** title.

I' the field prove flatterers, let courts and cities be
Made all of false-faced soothing. When steel grows   50
Soft as the parasite's silk, let him be made
An overture for the wars. No more, I say.
For that I have not washed my nose that bled,
Or foiled some debile wretch, which without note
Here's many else have done, you shout me forth   55
In acclamations hyperbolical,
As if I loved my little should be dieted
In praises sauced with lies.
   Com.   Too modest are you;
More cruel to your good report than grateful   60
To us that give you truly. By your patience,
If 'gainst yourself you be incensed, we'll put you—
Like one that means his proper harm—in manacles,
Then reason safely with you. Therefore be it known,
As to us, to all the world, that Caius Marcius   65
Wears this war's garland; in token of the which,
My noble steed, known to the camp, I give him,
With all his trim belonging; and from this time,
For what he did before Corioli, call him
With all the applause and clamor of the host,   70
Caius Marcius Coriolanus.
Bear the addition nobly ever!
          Flourish. Trumpets sound, and drums.
   All. Caius Marcius Coriolanus!
   Cor. I will go wash;
And when my face is fair you shall perceive   75
Whether I blush or no. Howbeit, I thank you;
I mean to stride your steed, and at all times

78. **undercrest your good addition:** take the title as my crest and bear myself in a manner worthy of it.

83. **us:** i.e., on our behalf.

84. **articulate:** come to terms.

91. **sometime:** once.

99. **Deliver:** release.

To undercrest your good addition
To the fairness of my power.

   Com.   So, to our tent;   80
Where, ere we do repose us, we will write
To Rome of our success. You, Titus Lartius,
Must to Corioli back. Send us to Rome
The best, with whom we may articulate
For their own good and ours.   85

   Lar.   I shall, my lord.

   Cor. The gods begin to mock me. I, that now
Refused most princely gifts, am bound to beg
Of my Lord General.

   Com.   Take 't; 'tis yours; what is't?   90

   Cor. I sometime lay here in Corioli
At a poor man's house; he used me kindly.
He cried to me; I saw him prisoner;
But then Aufidius was within my view,
And wrath o'erwhelmed my pity. I request you   95
To give my poor host freedom.

   Com.   O, well begged!
Were he the butcher of my son, he should
Be free as is the wind. Deliver him, Titus.

   Lar. Marcius, his name?   100

   Cor.   By Jupiter, forgot!
I am weary; yea, my memory is tired.
Have we no wine here?

   Com.   Go we to our tent.
The blood upon your visage dries; 'tis time   105
It should be looked to. Come.

                            Exeunt.

I. [x.] 4-5. I cannot/Being a Volsce, be that I am: i.e., being one of the defeated Volsces, I cannot be merciless as I would be in victory.

12. emulation: envy; see I. i. 235.

15. potch: thrust.

21. fly out of itself: cease to be the thing it is.

22. fane: temple; the authority of religion; **Capitol:** political power.

24. Embarquements: embargoes; restraints.

[Scene X. The camp of the Volsces.]

*A flourish. Cornets. Enter Tullus Aufidius bloody,
with two or three Soldiers.*

Auf. The town is ta'en.
1. Sol. 'Twill be delivered back on good condition.
Auf. Condition!
I would I were a Roman; for I cannot,
Being a Volsce, be that I am. Condition?　　　　　5
What good condition can a treaty find
I' the part that is at mercy? Five times, Marcius,
I have fought with thee; so often hast thou beat me;
And wouldst do so, I think, should we encounter
As often as we eat. By the elements,　　　　　10
If e'er again I meet him beard to beard,
He's mine or I am his. Mine emulation
Hath not that honor in't it had; for where
I thought to crush him in an equal force,
True sword to sword, I'll potch at him some way;　15
Or wrath or craft may get him.
1. Sol.　　　　　　　　　He's the devil.
Auf. Bolder, though not so subtle. My valor's
　　poisoned
With only suff'ring stain by him; for him　　　　20
Shall fly out of itself. Nor sleep nor sanctuary,
Being naked, sick, nor fane nor Capitol,
The prayers of priests nor times of sacrifice,
Embarquements all of fury, shall lift up
Their rotten privilege and custom 'gainst　　　　25

27. **upon my brother's guard:** protected by my brother.

28. **hospitable canon:** law of hospitality.

My hate to Marcius. Where I find him, were it
At home, upon my brother's guard, even there,
Against the hospitable canon, would I
Wash my fierce hand in's heart. Go you to the city;
Learn how 'tis held, and what they are that must   30
Be hostages for Rome.
    1. Sol.   Will not you go?
    Auf. I am attended at the cypress grove; I pray
        you—
'Tis south the city mills—bring me word thither   35
How the world goes, that to the pace of it
I may spur on my journey.
    1. Sol.   I shall, sir.

                                Exeunt.

THE TRAGEDY OF
CORIOLANUS

ACT II

II. Coriolanus, as he is henceforth to be known, is greeted with triumph in Rome but is impatient at hearing his praises voiced. The malicious tribunes of the people, Brutus and Sicinius, fear that Coriolanus will be granted a consulship, but are hopeful that his arrogance will spoil his chances. They know that he will not gracefully perform the ritual of asking the people for their suffrage. The nobility approve Coriolanus' appointment as consul and his friends persuade him to make the traditional gesture of asking the approval of individual plebeians. In doing so, however, he makes no secret of his distaste and his contempt for the citizens. The tribunes have no difficulty in swaying the people to change their minds.

⠀⠀⠀⠀⠀⠀|||||||||||||||||||||||||||||||||||

II.[i.]16-7. In what enormity is Marcius poor in that you two have not in abundance: what monstrous fault does Marcius lack that you two have not in great measure.

ACT II

[Scene I. Rome. A public place.]

*Enter Menenius, with the two Tribunes of the
people, Sicinius and Brutus.*

Men. The augurer tells me we shall have news tonight.

Bru. Good or bad?

Men. Not according to the prayer of the people, for
they love not Marcius.   5

Sic. Nature teaches beasts to know their friends.

Men. Pray you, who does the wolf love?

Sic. The lamb.

Men. Ay, to devour him, as the hungry plebeians
would the noble Marcius.   10

Bru. He's a lamb indeed, that baes like a bear.

Men. He's a bear indeed, that lives like a lamb. You
two are old men; tell me one thing that I shall ask
you.

Both Trib. Well, sir.   15

Men. In what enormity is Marcius poor in that you
two have not in abundance?

Bru. He's poor in no one fault, but stored with all.

Sic. Especially in pride.

Bru. And topping all others in boasting.   20

22-3. **us o' the right-hand file:** we in positions of honor; we upper-class folk.

28-9. **thief of occasion:** i.e., occasion (excuse) is the thief.

37. **single:** puny; contemptible.

47. **humorous:** whimsical.

49. **allaying Tiber:** diluting water.

Men. This is strange now. Do you two know how you are censured here in the city—I mean of us o' the right-hand file? Do you?

Both Trib. Why, how are we censured?

Men. Because you talk of pride now—will you not 25 be angry?

Both Trib. Well, well, sir, well.

Men. Why, 'tis no great matter; for a very little thief of occasion will rob you of a great deal of patience. Give your dispositions the reins, and be angry at 30 your pleasures—at the least, if you take it as a pleasure to you in being so. You blame Marcius for being proud?

Bru. We do it not alone, sir.

Men. I know you can do very little alone; for your 35 helps are many, or else your actions would grow wondrous single: your abilities are too infantlike for doing much alone. You talk of pride. O that you could turn your eyes toward the napes of your necks, and make but an interior survey of your good 40 selves! O that you could!

Both Trib. What then, sir?

Men. Why, then you should discover a brace of un-meriting, proud, violent, testy magistrates—alias fools —as any in Rome. 45

Sic. Menenius, you are known well enough too.

Men. I am known to be a humorous patrician, and one that loves a cup of hot wine with not a drop of allaying Tiber in't; said to be something im-perfect in favoring the first complaint, hasty and 50

51. **motion:** incitement.

55. **wealsmen:** statesmen; **Lycurguses:** lawgivers. Lycurgus was credited with creating the constitution of Sparta.

58. **delivered:** reported.

63-4. **map of my microcosm:** i.e., my face. Man was considered a **microcosm** as compared to the "macrocosm" (universe).

65. **bisson conspectuities:** blinded visions; faulty perceptions.

70-1. **caps and legs:** deference. "You want the common people to doff their caps and bow to you."

73. **fosset-seller:** seller of barrel taps; **rejourn:** adjourn; postpone.

77. **mummers:** pantomime actors.

78. **bloody flag:** standard of war.

tinderlike upon too trivial motion; one that con-
verses more with the buttock of the night than with
the forehead of the morning. What I think I utter,
and spend my malice in my breath. Meeting two such
wealsmen as you are—I cannot call you Lycurguses   55
—if the drink you give me touch my palate adversely,
I make a crooked face at it. I cannot say your
worships have delivered the matter well when I
find the ass in compound with the major part
of your syllables; and though I must be content   60
to bear with those that say you are reverend
grave men, yet they lie deadly that tell you you have
good faces. If you see this in the map of my microcosm, follows it that I am known well enough
too? What harm can your bisson conspectuities glean   65
out of this character, if I be known well enough
too?

Bru. Come, sir, come; we know you well enough.

Men. You know neither me, yourselves, nor any
thing. You are ambitious for poor knaves' caps   70
and legs; you wear out a good wholesome fore-
noon in hearing a cause between an orangewife
and a fosset-seller, and then rejourn the controversy of threepence to a second day of audience.
When you are hearing a matter between party   75
and party, if you chance to be pinched with the
colic, you make faces like mummers, set up the
bloody flag against all patience, and, in roaring
for a chamber pot, dismiss the controversy bleeding, the more entangled by your hearing. All the   80

84-5. a perfecter giber for the table than a necessary bencher in the Capitol: a better jester than a judge.

91. botcher: bungler; one who repairs clothes or shoes clumsily. Cushions were sometimes stuffed with hair.

94. Deucalion: the Greek mythological character who repopulated the earth after Jove's flood by casting on the ground stones which turned to men.

96. Godden: God give you good evening.

97. being: i.e., since you are.

106-7. most prosperous approbation: great success and applause.

Deucalion creating a new race of men. From Lodovico Dolce, *Le trasformationi* (1570).

peace you make in their cause is calling both the
parties knaves. You are a pair of strange ones.

Bru. Come, come, you are well understood to be
a perfecter giber for the table than a necessary
bencher in the Capitol.   85

Men. Our very priests must become mockers if they
shall encounter such ridiculous subjects as you are.
When you speak best unto the purpose, it is not
worth the wagging of your beards; and your beards
deserve not so honorable a grave as to stuff a   90
botcher's cushion or to be entombed in an ass's
packsaddle. Yet you must be saying Marcius is
proud, who, in a cheap estimation, is worth all
your predecessors since Deucalion; though per-
adventure some of the best of 'em were heredi-   95
tary hangmen. Godden to your worships. More
of your conversation would infect my brain, being
the herdsmen of the beastly plebeians. I will be
bold to take my leave of you.

> [*Brutus and Sicinius go aside.*]

Enter Volumnia, Virgilia, and Valeria.

How now, my as fair as noble ladies—and the   100
moon, were she earthly, no nobler—whither do you
follow your eyes so fast?

Vol. Honorable Menenius, my boy Marcius ap-
proaches; for the love of Juno, let's go.

Men. Ha! Marcius coming home?   105

Vol. Ay, worthy Menenius, and with most prosperous approbation.

108. **Take my cap, Jupiter ... Hoo:** Menenius throws up his cap to the god and shouts "hurrah" to acclaim Marcius' triumph.

118. **make a lip:** curl my lip in scorn.

119. **sovereign:** powerful; effective.

120. **Galen:** one of the most famous of ancient physicians, born in A.D. 129; **empiricutic:** quackish.

121. **drench:** medicinal draught.

135. **fidiused:** i.e., treated as Aufidius could expect to be treated by Marcius in a fight to the death.

136. **possessed:** informed.

A Roman wreath of victory. From Claude Guichard, *Funerailles et diverses manieres* (1581).

Men. Take my cap, Jupiter, and I thank thee. Hoo!
Marcius coming home!

Vol., Vir. Nay, 'tis true.   110

Vol. Look, here's a letter from him; the state hath
another, his wife another; and I think there's one
at home for you.

Men. I will make my very house reel tonight. A letter for me?   115

Vir. Yes, certain, there's a letter for you; I saw't.

Men. A letter for me! It gives me an estate of seven
years' health; in which time I will make a lip at
the physician. The most sovereign prescription in
Galen is but empiricutic and, to this preservative, 120
of no better report than a horse drench. Is he
not wounded? He was wont to come home
wounded.

Vir. O, no, no, no.

Vol. O, he is wounded, I thank the gods for't.   125

Men. So do I too, if it be not too much. Brings a
victory in his pocket? The wounds become him.

Vol. On's brows, Menenius; he comes the third
time home with the oaken garland.

Men. Has he disciplined Aufidius soundly?   130

Vol. Titus Lartius writes they fought together, but
Aufidius got off.

Men. And 'twas time for him too, I'll warrant him
that; an he had stayed by him, I would not have
been so fidiused for all the chests in Corioli and 135
the gold that's in them. Is the Senate possessed of
this?

140. **whole name of:** complete credit for.

142. **In troth:** truly.

145. **true purchasing:** honest acquiring.

147. **Pow, waw:** an exclamation of contempt at the very thought that the wondrous things might not be true.

150. **worships:** worthies; honored sirs.

155. **Tarquin:** as a youth Coriolanus had taken part in the defeat of the tyrant Tarquinius Superbus.

165. **nervy:** sinewy; powerful.

166. **declines:** falls.

Coriolanus and his mother. From Guillaume Rouillé, *Promptuarii iconum* (1553).

Vol. Good ladies, let's go. Yes, yes, yes: the Senate
has letters from the general, wherein he gives my
son the whole name of the war; he hath in this   140
action outdone his former deeds doubly.

Val. In troth, there's wondrous things spoke of
him.

Men. Wondrous! Ay, I warrant you, and not without his true purchasing.   145

Vir. The gods grant them true!

Vol. True! Pow, waw.

Men. True! I'll be sworn they are true. Where is
he wounded? [*To the Tribunes*] God save your
good worships! Marcius is coming home; he has   150
more cause to be proud. Where is he wounded?

Vol. I' the shoulder and i' the left arm; there will be
large cicatrices to show the people when he shall
stand for his place. He received in the repulse of
Tarquin seven hurts i' the body.   155

Men. One i' the neck and two i' the thigh—there's
nine that I know.

Vol. He had before this last expedition twenty-five
wounds upon him.

Men. Now it's twenty-seven; every gash was an   160
enemy's grave. (*A shout and flourish.*) Hark! The
trumpets.

Vol. These are the ushers of Marcius. Before him
he carries noise, and behind him he leaves tears;
Death, that dark spirit, in's nervy arm doth lie,   165
Which, being advanced, declines, and then men die.

*A sennet. Trumpets sound. Enter Cominius the
General, and Titus Lartius; between them, Coriolanus, crowned with an oaken garland; with Captains and Soldiers and a Herald.*

Her. Know, Rome, that all alone Marcius did fight
Within Corioli gates, where he hath won,
With fame, a name to Caius Marcius; these
In honor follows Coriolanus.   170
Welcome to Rome, renowned Coriolanus!   *Flourish.*
 All. Welcome to Rome, renowned Coriolanus!
 Cor. No more of this, it does offend my heart.
Pray now, no more.
 Com.   Look, sir, your mother!   —175
 Cor.   O,
You have, I know, petitioned all the gods
For my prosperity!   *Kneels.*
 Vol.   Nay, my good soldier, up;
My gentle Marcius, worthy Caius, and   180
By deed-achieving honor newly named—
What is it? Coriolanus must I call thee?
But, O, thy wife!
 Cor.   My gracious silence, hail!
Wouldst thou have laughed had I come coffined 185
    home,
That weepst to see me triumph? Ah, my dear,
Such eyes the widows in Corioli wear,
And mothers that lack sons.
 Men.   Now the gods crown thee! 190

197. **light and heavy:** merry and solemn.

201. **crab:** crab-apple.

203. **grafted to your relish:** improved by grafting to make them sweeter to the taste. That is, there are certain Romans who are unalterably sour towards Coriolanus.

216. **inherited:** possessed.

Cor. And live you yet? [*To Valeria*] O my sweet
    lady, pardon.

Vol. I know not where to turn.
O, welcome home! And welcome, General.
And y'are welcome all.   195

Men. A hundred thousand welcomes. I could weep
And I could laugh; I am light and heavy. Welcome!
A curse begin at very root on's heart
That is not glad to see thee! You are three
That Rome should dote on; yet, by the faith of men, 200
We have some old crab trees here at home that will
    not
Be grafted to your relish. Yet welcome, warriors.
We call a nettle but a nettle, and
The faults of fools but folly.   205

Com.   Ever right.

Cor. Menenius, ever, ever.

Her. Give way there, and go on.

Cor. [*To his wife and mother*] Your hand, and
    yours.   210
Ere in our own house I do shade my head,
The good patricians must be visited;
From whom I have received not only greetings,
But with them change of honors.

Vol.   I have lived   215
To see inherited my very wishes,
And the buildings of my fancy; only
There's one thing wanting, which I doubt not but
Our Rome will cast upon thee.

Cor.   Know, good mother, 220

221-22. **be . . . theirs:** serve them after my own fashion than rule them as they may choose.

226. **Your . . . nurse:** i.e., nurses as a class.

227. **rapture:** fit.

228. **chats him:** chats about him; **kitchen malkin:** scullery maid. **Malkin** was a diminutive used in contempt for girls of a low class.

229. **lockram:** fabric; **reechy:** greasy; dirty.

230. **stalls, bulks:** stands in the street for the display of merchants' wares.

232. **leads:** roofs, so called from the lead with which they were sheeted; **ridges horsed:** roof-ridges straddled.

233. **variable complexions:** people of varying types. **Complexions** refers to character or temperament, not personal appearance.

234. **Seld-shown flamens:** seldom-seen priests.

235. **popular:** common.

236. **vulgar station:** standing room among the vulgar.

237-39. **Commit the war of white and damask in/Their nicely gauded cheeks to the wanton spoil/Of Phoebus' burning kisses:** offer their cleverly painted red and white complexions to the mercy of the sun's rays; **pother:** commotion.

240-42. **As if that whatsoever god who leads him/Were slyly crept into his human powers,/And gave him graceful posture:** as if the divinity who governs Coriolanus had infused him and given him the attributes of a god.

247-48. **temp'rately transport his honors/From where he should begin and end:** carry off his honors modestly from first to last.

I had rather be their servant in my way
Then sway with them in theirs.

   Com.   On, to the Capitol.
       Flourish. Cornets. Exeunt in state, as before.

     Brutus and Sicinius [come forward].

   Bru. All tongues speak of him and the bleared
     sights   225
Are spectacled to see him. Your prattling nurse
Into a rapture lets her baby cry
While she chats him; the kitchen malkin pins
Her richest lockram 'bout her reechy neck,
Clamb'ring the walls to eye him; stalls, bulks, win- 230
    dows,
Are smothered up, leads filled and ridges horsed
With variable complexions, all agreeing
In earnestness to see him. Seld-shown flamens
Do press among the popular throngs and puff   235
To win a vulgar station; our veiled dames
Commit the war of white and damask in
Their nicely gauded cheeks to the wanton spoil
Of Phoebus' burning kisses. Such a pother,
As if that whatsoever god who leads him   240
Were slyly crept into his human powers,
And gave him graceful posture.
   Sic.   On the sudden
I warrant him consul.
   Bru.   Then our office may   245
During his power go sleep.
   Sic. He cannot temp'rately transport his honors

254. **which:** i.e., which cause.

260. **napless vesture:** worn garment. It was customary for applicants for office to humble themselves by wearing modest clothing.

262. **breaths:** voices approving his election as consul.

276. **still:** always.

278. **Dispropertied their freedoms:** deprived them of their liberties.

From where he should begin and end but will
Lose those he hath won.

    Bru.   In that there's comfort. 250
    Sic.   Doubt not
The commoners, for whom we stand, but they
Upon their ancient malice will forget
With the least cause these his new honors; which
That he will give them make I as little question 255
As he is proud to do't.

    Bru.   I heard him swear,
Were he to stand for consul, never would he
Appear i' the market place, nor on him put
The napless vesture of humility; 260
Nor, showing, as the manner is, his wounds
To the people, beg their stinking breaths.

    Sic.   'Tis right.
    Bru. It was his word. O, he would miss it rather
Than carry it but by the suit of the gentry to him 265
And the desire of the nobles.

    Sic.   I wish no better
Than have him hold that purpose and to put it
In execution.

    Bru.   'Tis most like he will. 270
    Sic. It shall be to him then as our good wills:
A sure destruction.

    Bru.   So it must fall out
To him or our authorities. For an end,
We must suggest the people in what hatred 275
He still hath held them; that to's power he would
Have made them mules, silenced their pleaders, and
Dispropertied their freedoms, holding them

281. **provand:** provender; feed.
287. **put upon't:** incited to it.
302. **the time:** the present happening.
303. **event:** ultimate outcome.
304. **Have with you:** let's go.

In human action and capacity
Of no more soul nor fitness for the world   280
Than camels in their war, who have their provand
Only for bearing burdens and sore blows
For sinking under them.
   Sic.   This, as you say, suggested
At some time when his soaring insolence   285
Shall touch the people—which time shall not want,
If he be put upon't, and that's as easy
As to set dogs on sheep—will be his fire
To kindle their dry stubble; and their blaze
Shall darken him forever.   290

Enter a Messenger.

   Bru.   What's the matter?
   Mess. You are sent for to the Capitol. 'Tis thought
That Marcius shall be consul.
I have seen the dumb men throng to see him and
The blind to hear him speak; matrons flung gloves,   295
Ladies and maids their scarfs and handkerchers,
Upon him as he passed; the nobles bended
As to Jove's statue, and the commons made
A shower and thunder with their caps and shouts.
I never saw the like.   300
   Bru.   Let's to the Capitol,
And carry with us ears and eyes for the time,
But hearts for the event.
   Sic.   Have with you.
                            Exeunt.

II. [ii.] 5. vengeance: excessively; compare the phrase "with a vengeance."

20. discover: reveal.

21. opposite: enemy; **affect:** seek.

· C A P I T O L I V M ·

The Capitol. From Giovanni Bartolommeo Marliani, *Urbis Romae topographia* (1588).

[Scene II. The same. The Capitol.]

*Enter two Officers, to lay cushions, as it
were in the Capitol.*

1. Off. Come, come, they are almost here. How
many stand for consulships?

2. Off. Three, they say; but 'tis thought of every
one Coriolanus will carry it.

1. Off. That's a brave fellow; but he's vengeance   5
proud and loves not the common people.

2. Off. Faith, there have been many great men that
have flattered the people who ne'er loved them; and
there be many that they have loved they know not
wherefore; so that, if they love they know not why,   10
they hate upon no better a ground. Therefore, for
Coriolanus neither to care whether they love or hate
him manifests the true knowledge he has in their disposition, and out of his noble carelessness lets them
plainly see't.   15

1. Off. If he did not care whether he had their love
or no, he waved indifferently 'twixt doing them neither good nor harm; but he seeks their hate with
greater devotion than they can render it him and
leaves nothing undone that may fully discover him   20
their opposite. Now to seem to affect the malice and
displeasure of the people is as bad as that which he
dislikes, to flatter them for their love.

2. Off. He hath deserved worthily of his country;

27. **bonneted:** i.e., won favor by being deferential.

28. **estimation and report:** popularity.

Ent. after l. 36. **Lictors:** attendants of Roman magistrates whose function was to clear the path before them.

37. **determined of:** decided about.

40. **gratify:** reward.

44. **well-found successes:** successes which clearly deserve to be so called.

48. **like himself:** worthy of him.

and his ascent is not by such easy degrees as those   25
who, having been supple and courteous to the people,
bonneted, without any further deed to have them at
all, into their estimation and report; but he hath so
planted his honors in their eyes and his actions in
their hearts that for their tongues to be silent and not   30
confess so much were a kind of ingrateful injury; to
report otherwise were a malice that, giving itself the
lie, would pluck reproof and rebuke from every ear
that heard it.

    1. Off. No more of him; he's a worthy man. Make   35
way, they are coming.

*A sennet. Enter the Patricians and the Tribunes of the
People, Lictors before them; Coriolanus, Menenius,
Cominius the Consul. Sicinius and Brutus take their
    places by themselves. Coriolanus stands.*

    Men. Having determined of the Volsces, and
To send for Titus Lartius, it remains,
As the main point of this our after-meeting,
To gratify his noble service that   40
Hath thus stood for his country. Therefore, please you,
Most reverend and grave elders, to desire
The present consul and last general
In our well-found successes to report
A little of that worthy work performed   45
By Caius Marcius Coriolanus; whom
We met here both to thank and to remember
With honors like himself.   *[Coriolanus sits.]*

51-2. Rather our state's defective for requital /Than we to stretch it out: i.e., we are rather deficient in the means to compensate Coriolanus adequately than in the will to do so.

52. Masters o' the people: addressed to the tribunes.

54-5. Your loving motion toward the common body,/To yield what passes here: your favorable report to the people regarding the proposals we make.

56. convented: convened.

57. Upon a pleasing treaty: for consideration of a pleasing proposal.

59. theme: i.e., Coriolanus.

61. blessed: happy.

64. off: irrelevant.

1. Sen.   Speak, good Cominius.
Leave nothing out for length, and make us think   50
Rather our state's defective for requital
Than we to stretch it out. Masters o' the people,
We do request your kindest ears; and, after,
Your loving motion toward the common body,
To yield what passes here.   55
Sic.   We are convented
Upon a pleasing treaty, and have hearts
Inclinable to honor and advance
The theme of our assembly.
Bru.   Which the rather   60
We shall be blessed to do, if he remember
A kinder value of the people than
He hath hereto prized them at.
Men.   That's off, that's off;
I would you rather had been silent. Please you   65
To hear Cominius speak?
Bru.   Most willingly.
But yet my caution was more pertinent
Than the rebuke you give it.
Men.   He loves your people;   70
But tie him not to be their bedfellow.
Worthy Cominius, speak.
                    Coriolanus rises, and offers to go away.
Nay, keep your place.
1. Sen. Sit, Coriolanus, never shame to hear
What you have nobly done.   75
Cor.   Your Honors' pardon.
I had rather have my wounds to heal again
Than hear say how I got them.

80. **disbenched:** i.e., stirred him to rise.

83. **soothed:** flattered; see **soothing,** I.[ix.]50.

89. **monstered:** displayed as wonders.

92. **That's thousand to one good one:** among whom (the **multiplying spawn**) there is only one good man in a thousand.

94. **one on's ears to hear it:** i.e., that one of his ears should hear his honor praised.

100. **Be singly counterpoised:** be matched by any one man.

101. **made a head for:** attacked with an army.

104. **Amazonian:** beardless, like an Amazon.

105-6. **bestrid/An o'erpressed Roman:** straddled the body of a prostrate Roman and fought in his defense.

108. **on his knee:** to his knees.

The expulsion of Tarquinius Superbus. From **Livy,** *Historicus duobus libri auctos* (1520).

Bru.   Sir, I hope
My words disbenched you not.   80
    Cor.   No, sir; yet oft,
When blows have made me stay, I fled from words.
You soothed not, therefore hurt not. But your people,
I love them as they weigh—
    Men.   Pray now, sit down.   85
    Cor. I had rather have one scratch my head i' the
        sun
When the alarum were struck than idly sit
To hear my nothings monstered.   *Exit.*
    Men.   Masters of the people, 90
Your multiplying spawn how can he flatter—
That's thousand to one good one—when you now see
He had rather venture all his limbs for honor
Than one on's ears to hear it? Proceed, Cominius.
    Com. I shall lack voice; the deeds of Coriolanus   95
Should not be uttered feebly. It is held
That valor is the chiefest virtue and
Most dignifies the haver. If it be,
The man I speak of cannot in the world
Be singly counterpoised. At sixteen years,   100
When Tarquin made a head for Rome, he fought
Beyond the mark of others; our then dictator,
Whom with all praise I point at, saw him fight
When with his Amazonian chin he drove
The bristled lips before him; he bestrid   105
An o'erpressed Roman and i' the consul's view
Slew three opposers; Tarquin's self he met,
And struck him on his knee. In that day's feats,
When he might act the woman in the scene,

110. **meed:** reward.

111-12. **His pupil age/Man-ent'red:** his apprenticeship begun in manly fashion; **waxed:** grew.

114. **lurched all swords of the garland:** won the victor's wreath from all other soldiers.

116. **speak him home:** describe him thoroughly; do full justice to his virtues.

120. **stem:** prow.

124. **mortal:** deadly; i.e., which it should have been death to enter.

126-27. **struck/. . . like a planet:** blasted. Planets were credited with destructive influence, as stars are still believed by some to influence men's fortunes.

130. **fatigate:** fatigued.

132. **reeking:** smelling of blood.

137. **with measure:** proportionately; adequately.

He proved best man i' the field, and for his meed   110
Was brow-bound with the oak. His pupil age
Man-ent'red thus, he waxed like a sea,
And in the brunt of seventeen battles since
He lurched all swords of the garland. For this last,
Before and in Corioli, let me say   115
I cannot speak him home. He stopped the fliers,
And by his rare example made the coward
Turn terror into sport; as weeds before
A vessel under sail, so men obeyed
And fell below his stem. His sword, death's stamp,   120
Where it did mark, it took; from face to foot
He was a thing of blood, whose every motion
Was timed with dying cries. Alone he ent'red
The mortal gate of the city, which he painted
With shunless destiny; aidless came off,   125
And with a sudden reinforcement struck
Corioli like a planet. Now all's his.
When by and by the din of war 'gan pierce
His ready sense, then straight his doubled spirit
Requick'ned what in flesh was fatigate,   130
And to the battle came he; where he did
Run reeking o'er the lives of men as if
'Twere a perpetual spoil; and till we called
Both field and city ours he never stood
To ease his breast with panting.   135
   Men.   Worthy man!
   1. Sen. He cannot but with measure fit the honors
Which we devise him.
   Com.   Our spoils he kicked at,
And looked upon things precious as they were   140

142-44. **misery:** miserliness; **rewards/His deeds with doing them, and is content/To spend the time to end it:** i.e., to him the opportunity for noble deeds is its own reward and action alone is enough to content him.

161. **bate:** omit.

163. **Put them not to't:** don't anger them.

166. **with your form:** with the traditional formalities.

The common muck of the world. He covets less
Than misery itself would give, rewards
His deeds with doing them, and is content
To spend the time to end it.

   Men.   He's right noble;   **145**
Let him be called for.

   1. Sen.   Call Coriolanus.

   Off. He doth appear.

         [Re-]enter Coriolanus.

   Men. The Senate, Coriolanus, are well pleased
To make thee consul.   **150**

   Cor.   I do owe them still
My life and services.

   Men.   It then remains
That you do speak to the people.

   Cor.   I do beseech you   **155**
Let me o'erleap that custom; for I cannot
Put on the gown, stand naked, and entreat them
For my wounds' sake to give their suffrage. Please you
That I may pass this doing.

   Sic.   Sir, the people   **160**
Must have their voices; neither will they bate
One jot of ceremony.

   Men.   Put them not to't.
Pray you go fit you to the custom, and
Take to you, as your predecessors have,   **165**
Your honor with your form.

   Cor.   It is a part

174. **breath:** approval, as at II.[i.]262.

176-77. **We recommend to you . . ./Our purpose to them:** we submit to you the announcement to the people of our purpose.

181. **require:** ask.

▲FORVM▲ ROMANVM▲

The Forum. From Giovanni Bartolommeo Marliani, *Urbis Romae topographia* (1588).

That I shall blush in acting, and might well
Be taken from the people.

    Bru.   Mark you that?   170

    Cor. To brag unto them, "Thus I did, and thus!"
Show them the unaching scars which I should hide,
As if I had received them for the hire
Of their breath only!

    Men.   Do not stand upon't.   175
We recommend to you, tribunes of the people,
Our purpose to them; and to our noble consul
Wish we all joy and honor.

    Sen. To Coriolanus come all joy and honor!

Flourish. Cornets. Then exeunt [all but Sicinius and
Brutus.]

    Bru. You see how he intends to use the people.   180

    Sic. May they perceive's intent! He will require
    them
As if he did contemn what he requested
Should be in them to give.

    Bru.   Come, we'll inform them 185
Of our proceedings here. On the market place
I know they do attend us.

                         Exeunt.

[Scene III. The same. The Forum.]

Enter seven or eight Citizens.

    1. Cit. Once, if he do require our voices, we ought
not to deny him.

    2. Cit. We may, sir, if we will.

    3. Cit. We have power in ourselves to do it, but it

II. [**iii.**] 19. **abram:** auburn.

23. **consent of one direct way:** agreement to follow one direction.

34. **you may:** i.e., you may have your little joke.

is a power that we have no power to do; for if he   5
show us his wounds and tell us his deeds, we are to
put our tongues into those wounds and speak for
them; so, if he tell us his noble deeds, we must also
tell him our noble acceptance of them. Ingratitude is
monstrous, and for the multitude to be ingrateful   10
were to make a monster of the multitude; of the
which we being members should bring ourselves to
be monstrous members.

1. Cit. And to make us no better thought of, a little
help will serve; for once we stood up about the corn,   15
he himself stuck not to call us the many-headed multitude.

3. Cit. We have been called so of many; not that
our heads are some brown, some black, some abram,
some bald, but that our wits are so diversely colored;   20
and truly I think if all our wits were to issue out of
one skull, they would fly east, west, north, south, and
their consent of one direct way should be at once to
all the points o' the compass.

2. Cit. Think you so? Which way do you judge my   25
wit would fly?

3. Cit. Nay, your wit will not so soon out as another
man's will—'tis strongly wedged up in a blockhead;
but if it were at liberty 'twould sure southward.

2. Cit. Why that way?   30

3. Cit. To lose itself in a fog; where being three
parts melted away with rotten dews, the fourth would
return for conscience' sake, to help to get thee a wife.

2. Cit. You are never without your tricks; you may,
you may.   35

43. by particulars: person by person; of each citizen individually.

60-1. like the virtues/Which our divines lose by 'em: as they forget the virtues that our divines try vainly to instill in them.

3. *Cit.* Are you all resolved to give your voices? But that's no matter, the greater part carries it. I say, if he would incline to the people, there was never a worthier man.

*Enter Coriolanus, in a gown of humility,
with Menenius.*

Here he comes, and in the gown of humility. Mark 40
his behavior. We are not to stay all together, but to
come by him where he stands, by ones, by twos, and
by threes. He's to make his requests by particulars,
wherein every one of us has a single honor, in giving
him our own voices with our own tongues; therefore 45
follow me, and I'll direct you how you shall go by him.

All. Content, content. [*Exeunt Citizens.*]

Men. O sir, you are not right; have you not known
The worthiest men have done't?

Cor. What must I say? 50
"I pray, sir"—Plague upon't! I cannot bring
My tongue to such a pace. "Look, sir, my wounds!
I got them in my country's service, when
Some certain of your brethren roared and ran
From the noise of our own drums." 55

Men. O me, the gods!
You must not speak of that. You must desire them
To think upon you.

Cor. Think upon me? Hang 'em!
I would they would forget me, like the virtues 60
Which our divines lose by 'em.

84. A match: agreed; that's that.

Men.   You'll mar all.
I'll leave you. Pray you speak to 'em, I pray you,
In wholesome manner.   *Exit.*

[Re-]*enter three of the Citizens.*

Cor.   Bid them wash their faces   65
And keep their teeth clean. So, here comes a brace.
You know the cause, sir, of my standing here.

3. Cit. We do, sir; tell us what hath brought you
to't.

Cor. Mine own desert.   70

2. Cit. Your own desert?

Cor. Ay, not mine own desire.

3. Cit. How, not your own desire?

Cor. No, sir, 'twas never my desire yet to trouble
the poor with begging.   75

3. Cit. You must think, if we give you anything,
we hope to gain by you.

Cor. Well then, I pray, your price o' the consulship?

1. Cit. The price is to ask it kindly.

Cor. Kindly, sir, I pray let me ha't. I have wounds   80
to show you, which shall be yours in private. Your
good voice, sir; what say you?

2. Cit. You shall ha' it, worthy sir.

Cor. A match, sir. There's in all two worthy voices
begged. I have your alms. Adieu.   85

3. Cit. But this is something odd.

2. Cit. An 'twere to give again—but 'tis no matter.
                    Exeunt [*the three Citizens*].

88-9. **stand with the tune of your voices:** accord with your liking.

104-5. **popular man:** man who seeks popular approval.

111. **seal:** confirm.

[Re-]enter two other Citizens.

Cor. Pray you now, if it may stand with the tune of
your voices that I may be consul, I have here the customary gown.   90

4. Cit. You have deserved nobly of your country,
and you have not deserved nobly.

Cor. Your enigma?

4. Cit. You have been a scourge to her enemies; you
have been a rod to her friends. You have not indeed   95
loved the common people.

Cor. You should account me the more virtuous that
I have not been common in my love. I will, sir, flatter
my sworn brother, the people, to earn a dearer estimation of them; 'tis a condition they account gentle; and 100
since the wisdom of their choice is rather to have my
hat than my heart, I will practice the insinuating nod
and be off to them most counterfeitly. That is, sir, I
will counterfeit the bewitchment of some popular
man and give it bountiful to the desirers. Therefore, 105
beseech you I may be consul.

5. Cit. We hope to find you our friend; and therefore give you our voices heartily.

4. Cit. You have received many wounds for your
country.   110

Cor. I will not seal your knowledge with showing
them. I will make much of your voices, and so trouble
you no farther.

Both Cit. The gods give you joy, sir, heartily!
                                            [Exeunt Citizens.]

118. **wolvish toge:** i.e., hypocritical humility, like the wolf in sheep's clothing. Steevens suggested **toge** in place of the First Folio's "tongue"; the later Folios change to "gowne."

128. **mo:** more.

130. **Watched:** spent sleepless nights.

Cor. Most sweet voices!   115
Better it is to die, better to starve,
Than crave the hire which first we do deserve.
Why in this wolvish toge should I stand here
To beg of Hob and Dick that do appear
Their needless vouches? Custom calls me to't.   120
What custom wills, in all things should we do't,
The dust on antique time would lie unswept,
And mountainous error be too highly heaped
For truth to o'erpeer. Rather than fool it so,
Let the high office and the honor go   125
To one that would do thus. I am half through:
The one part suffered, the other will I do.

Enter three Citizens more.

Here come mo voices.
Your voices. For your voices I have fought;
Watched for your voices; for your voices bear   130
Of wounds two dozen odd; battles thrice six
I have seen and heard of; for your voices have
Done many things, some less, some more. Your voices?
Indeed, I would be consul.

  6. Cit. He has done nobly, and cannot go without   135
any honest man's voice.

  7. Cit. Therefore let him be consul. The gods give
him joy, and make him good friend to the people!

  All. Amen, amen. God save thee, noble consul!
                              [*Exeunt Citizens.*]
Cor. Worthy voices!   140

143. **Endue:** endow; **Remains:** all that remains is.

144. **official marks:** i.e., the robes of office.

149. **upon your approbation:** for confirmation of your appointment.

161. **warm at's heart:** a source of satisfaction to him.

163. **weeds:** garments.

[Re-]enter Menenius with Brutus and Sicinius.

Men. You have stood your limitation, and the trib-
    unes
Endue you with the people's voice. Remains
That, in the official marks invested, you
Anon do meet the Senate.   145
    Cor.   Is this done?
    Sic. The custom of request you have discharged.
The people do admit you, and are summoned
To meet anon, upon your approbation.
    Cor. Where? At the Senate House?   150
    Sic.   There, Coriolanus.
    Cor. May I change these garments?
    Sic.   You may, sir.
    Cor. That I'll straight do, and, knowing myself
    again,   155
Repair to the Senate House.
    Men. I'll keep you company. Will you along?
    Bru. We stay here for the people.
    Sic.   Fare you well.
           Exeunt Coriolanus and Menenius.
He has it now; and by his looks methinks   160
'Tis warm at's heart.
    Bru. With a proud heart he wore
His humble weeds. Will you dismiss the people?

[Re-enter Citizens.]

    Sic. How now, my masters! Have you chose this
    man?   165

193. lessoned: coached.

1. Cit. He has our voices, sir.

Bru. We pray the gods he may deserve your loves.

2. Cit. Amen, sir. To my poor unworthy notice,
He mocked us when he begged our voices.

3. Cit.   Certainly;   170
He flouted us downright.

1. Cit. No, 'tis his kind of speech; he did not mock
    us.

2. Cit. Not one amongst us, save yourself, but says
He used us scornfully. He should have showed us   175
His marks of merit, wounds received for's country.

Sic. Why, so he did, I am sure.

All. No, no; no man saw 'em.

3. Cit. He said he had wounds which he could show
    in private,   180
And with his hat, thus waving it in scorn,
"I would be consul," says he; "aged custom
But by your voices will not so permit me;
Your voices therefore." When we granted that,
Here was, "I thank you for your voices. Thank you,   185
Your most sweet voices. Now you have left your
    voices,
I have no further with you." Was not this mockery?

Sic. Why either were you ignorant to see't,
Or, seeing it, of such childish friendliness   190
To yield your voices?

Bru.   Could you not have told him—
As you were lessoned—when he had no power
But was a petty servant to the state,
He was your enemy; ever spake against   195

197. **weal:** commonwealth.
203. **what he stood for:** the consulship.
208. **touched:** tested.
213. **article:** condition; terms.
218. **free:** open; unconcealed.
222. **heart:** courage.
223. **rectorship:** rule; **judgment:** wisdom.

Your liberties and the charters that you bear
I' the body of the weal; and now, arriving
A place of potency and sway o' the state,
If he should still malignantly remain
Fast foe to the plebeii, your voices might   200
Be curses to yourselves? You should have said
That as his worthy deeds did claim no less
Than what he stood for, so his gracious nature
Would think upon you for your voices, and
Translate his malice towards you into love,   205
Standing your friendly lord.

  Sic.   Thus to have said,
As you were foreadvised, had touched his spirit
And tried his inclination; from him plucked
Either his gracious promise, which you might,   210
As cause had called you up, have held him to;
Or else it would have galled his surly nature,
Which easily endures not article
Tying him to aught. So, putting him to rage,
You should have ta'en the advantage of his choler   215
And passed him unelected.

  Bru.   Did you perceive
He did solicit you in free contempt
When he did need your loves; and do you think
That his contempt shall not be bruising to you   220
When he hath power to crush? Why, had your bodies
No heart among you? Or had you tongues to cry
Against the rectorship of judgment?

  Sic.   Have you
Ere now denied the asker, and now again,   225

232. **piece:** add to.

240. **Enforce:** insist upon; emphasize.

245. **portance:** behavior.

249-51. **we labored,/No impediment between, but that you must/Cast your election on him:** we did all in our power to see that nothing prevented your electing him.

Of him that did not ask but mock, bestow
Your sued-for tongues?

   3. Cit. He's not confirmed: we may deny him yet.

   2. Cit. And will deny him;
I'll have five hundred voices of that sound.   230

   1. Cit. I twice five hundred, and their friends to
     piece 'em.

   Bru. Get you hence instantly, and tell those friends
They have chose a consul that will from them take
Their liberties, make them of no more voice   235
Than dogs, that are as often beat for barking
As therefore kept to do so.

   Sic.   Let them assemble;
And, on a safer judgment, all revoke
Your ignorant election. Enforce his pride   240
And his old hate unto you; besides, forget not
With what contempt he wore the humble weed;
How in his suit he scorned you; but your loves,
Thinking upon his services, took from you
The apprehension of his present portance,   245
Which, most gibingly, ungravely, he did fashion
After the inveterate hate he bears you.

   Bru.   Lay
A fault on us, your tribunes, that we labored,
No impediment between, but that you must   250
Cast your election on him.

   Sic.   Say you chose him
More after our commandment than as guided
By your own true affections; and that your minds,
Preoccupied with what you rather must do   255

262. **Ancus Marcius,** et al.: all more or less mythical figures.

266-67. **[Censorinus,] nobly named so,/Twice being [by the people chosen] censor:** the bracketed words do not appear in the Folio and are conjectural.

273. **Scaling:** balancing in the scales.

275. **sudden:** hasty.

278. **drawn your number:** gathered sufficient support.

Than what you should, made you against the grain
To voice him consul. Lay the fault on us.

  Bru. Ay, spare us not. Say we read lectures to you,
How youngly he began to serve his country,
How long continued; and what stock he springs of— 260
The noble house o' the Marcians; from whence came
That Ancus Marcius, Numa's daughter's son,
Who, after great Hostilius, here was king;
Of the same house Publius and Quintus were,
That our best water brought by conduits hither;   265
And [Censorinus,] nobly named so,
Twice being [by the people chosen] censor,
Was his great ancestor.

  Sic.   One thus descended,
That hath beside well in his person wrought   270
To be set high in place, we did commend
To your remembrances; but you have found,
Scaling his present bearing with his past,
That he's your fixed enemy, and revoke
Your sudden approbation.   275

  Bru.   Say you ne'er had done't—
Harp on that still—but by our putting on;
And presently, when you have drawn your number,
Repair to the Capitol.

  Cit.   We will so; almost all   280
Repent in their election.   *Exeunt [Citizens].*

  Bru.   Let them go on;
This mutiny were better put in hazard
Than stay, past doubt, for greater.
If, as his nature is, he fall in rage   285

With their refusal, both observe and answer
The vantage of his anger.

  Sic.   To the Capitol, come.
We will be there before the stream o' the people;
And this shall seem, as partly 'tis, their own,   290
Which we have goaded onward.

                              Exeunt.

THE TRAGEDY OF
CORIOLANUS

ACT III

III. When Coriolanus learns of the citizens' change of heart, he plays into the hands of the tribunes, raging against the folly of letting ignorant plebeians have a voice in the government. Brutus and Sicinius accuse him of treason and peremptorily order the ædiles to seize him and throw him to his death from the Tarpeian rock. With the help of the patricians, Coriolanus beats off the people and their ædiles and retires to the house of Menenius. Volumnia, his mother, although she is as proud and arrogant as Coriolanus himself, persuades him to relent and humble himself to the people and their tribunes. The tribunes, however, are determined to force his death or exile. Relying on their knowledge of his nature, they call him "traitor" and thus provoke another outburst which results in Coriolanus' banishment. Declaring that it is he who banishes Rome, he prepares to leave the city amid the cheers and jeers of the populace.

‖‖‖‖‖‖‖‖‖‖‖‖‖‖‖‖‖‖‖‖‖‖‖‖‖‖‖‖

III.[i.] 1. made new head: raised a new army.

3. composition: settlement (of peace terms).

11. On safeguard: accompanied by a protective guard.

ACT III

[Scene I. Rome. A street.]

Cornets. Enter Coriolanus, Menenius, all the Gentry,
Cominius, Titus Lartius, and other Senators.

  Cor. Tullus Aufidius, then, had made new head?
  Lar. He had, my lord; and that it was which caused
Our swifter composition.
  Cor. So then the Volsces stand but as at first,
Ready, when time shall prompt them, to make road   5
Upon's again.
  Com.   They are worn, Lord Consul, so
That we shall hardly in our ages see
Their banners wave again.
  Cor.   Saw you Aufidius?   10
  Lar. On safeguard he came to me, and did curse
Against the Volsces, for they had so vilely
Yielded the town. He is retired to Antium.
  Cor. Spoke he of me?
  Lar.   He did, my lord.   15
  Cor.   How? What?
  Lar. How often he had met you, sword to sword;
That of all things upon the earth he hated

28. prank them: dress themselves.

Your person most; that he would pawn his fortunes
To hopeless restitution, so he might   20
Be called your vanquisher.
   Cor. At Antium lives he?
   Lar. At Antium.
   Cor. I wish I had a cause to seek him there,
To oppose his hatred fully. Welcome home.   25

Enter Sicinius and Brutus.

Behold, these are the tribunes of the people,
The tongues o' the common mouth. I do despise them,
For they do prank them in authority,
Against all noble sufferance.
   Sic.   Pass no further.   30
   Cor. Ha! What is that?
   Bru. It will be dangerous to go on—no further.
   Cor. What makes this change?
   Men. The matter?
   Com. Hath he not passed the noble and the com-   35
    mon?
   Bru. Cominius, no.
   Cor.   Have I had children's voices?
   1. Sen. Tribunes, give way: he shall to the market
    place.   40
   Bru. The people are incensed against him.
   Sic.   Stop,
Or all will fall in broil.
   Cor.   Are these your herd?
Must these have voices, that can yield them now   45

53. **Suffer't:** allow it.

58. **Scandaled:** slandered.

62. **sithence:** since.

64. **like:** likely.

65-6. **Not unlike/Each way to better yours:** i.e., apt to do better than you in any business that concerns the people.

And straight disclaim their tongues? What are your
    offices?
You being their mouths, why rule you not their teeth?
Have you not set them on?

    Men.   Be calm, be calm.   50

    Cor. It is a purposed thing, and grows by plot,
To curb the will of the nobility;
Suffer't, and live with such as cannot rule
Nor ever will be ruled.

    Bru.   Call't not a plot.   55
The people cry you mocked them; and of late,
When corn was given them gratis, you repined;
Scandaled the suppliants for the people, called them
Time-pleasers, flatterers, foes to nobleness.

    Cor. Why, this was known before.   60
    Bru.   Not to them all.
    Cor. Have you informed them sithence?
    Bru.   How? I inform them!
    Com. You are like to do such business.
    Bru.   Not unlike   65
Each way to better yours.

    Cor. Why then should I be consul? By yond clouds,
Let me deserve so ill as you, and make me
Your fellow tribune.

    Sic.   You show too much of that   70
For which the people stir; if you will pass
To where you are bound, you must inquire your way,
Which you are out of, with a gentler spirit,
Or never be so noble as a consul,
Nor yoke with him for tribune.   75

    Men.   Let's be calm.

77. **abused:** deceived; **palt'ring:** haggling.
79. **dishonored rub:** dishonorable obstacle.
84. **heat:** anger.
87. **meinie:** herd.
91. **cockle:** weed.
103. **tetter:** infect with a skin eruption.

 Com. The people are abused; set on. This palt'ring
Becomes not Rome; nor has Coriolanus
Deserved this so dishonored rub, laid falsely
I' the plain way of his merit.   80
 Cor.   Tell me of corn!
This was my speech, and I will speak't again—
 Men. Not now, not now.
 1. Sen.   Not in this heat, sir, now.
 Cor. Now, as I live, I will.   85
My nobler friends, I crave their pardons.
For the mutable, rank-scented meinie, let them
Regard me as I do not flatter, and
Therein behold themselves. I say again,
In soothing them we nourish 'gainst our Senate 90
The cockle of rebellion, insolence, sedition,
Which we ourselves have plowed for, sowed, and
  scattered,
By mingling them with us, the honored number,
Who lack not virtue, no, nor power, but that 95
Which they have given to beggars.
 Men.   Well, no more.
 1. Sen. No more words, we beseech you.
 Cor.   How! no more!
As for my country I have shed my blood,   100
Not fearing outward force, so shall my lungs
Coin words till their decay against those measles
Which we disdain should tetter us, yet sought
The very way to catch them.
 Bru.   You speak o' the people 105
As if you were a god to punish, not
A man of their infirmity.

118. **Triton:** a sea god.

120. **from the canon:** i.e., Sicinius exceeds his authority in stating positively that Coriolanus **shall** be silenced.

124. **Hydra:** a monster of many heads; i.e., the populace.

129. **vail your ignorance:** make your ignorance (that gave him power) humble itself to him.

129-30. **awake/Your dangerous lenity:** arouse yourselves to an awareness of the danger that your lenience creates.

132. **have cushions by you:** i.e., share your rule of the commonwealth; sit on cushions as was the custom of senators.

133. **no less:** that is, no less than senators.

134-35. **the great'st taste/Most palates theirs:** the principal savor of any decision accords with their palates; their pleasure is decisive.

Hydra. From Claude Menestrier, *L'art des emblemes* (1684).

Sic.   'Twere well
We let the people know't.
   Men.   What, what? his choler?   110
   Cor. Choler!
Were I as patient as the midnight sleep,
By Jove, 'twould be my mind!
   Sic.   It is a mind
That shall remain a poison where it is,   115
Not poison any further.
   Cor.   Shall remain!
Hear you this Triton of the minnows? Mark you
His absolute "shall"?
   Com.   'Twas from the canon.   120
   Cor.   "Shall"!
O good but most unwise patricians! Why,
You grave but reckless senators, have you thus
Given Hydra here to choose an officer
That with his peremptory "shall," being but   125
The horn and noise o' the monster's, wants not spirit
To say he'll turn your current in a ditch,
And make your channel his? If he have power,
Then vail your ignorance; if none, awake
Your dangerous lenity. If you are learned,   130
Be not as common fools; if you are not,
Let them have cushions by you. You are plebeians
If they be senators; and they are no less,
When, both your voices blended, the great'st taste
Most palates theirs. They choose their magistrate;   135
And such a one as he, who puts his "shall,"
His popular "shall," against a graver bench
Than ever frowned in Greece. By Jove himself,

160. **thread the gates:** pass through the gates (to encounter the enemy).

165. **All cause unborn:** without any cause; **native:** natural result. This word has troubled editors, who since Johnson have amended it to "motive." But **native** probably is correct. In *The London Shakespeare*, John Munro comments: "To say that one thing is native to another is to say that one is related to the other in a natural and appropriate way, or is in some sense akin or compatible."

167. **this bosom multiplied:** these multiple hearts (of the people).

It makes the consuls base; and my soul aches
To know, when two authorities are up,   140
Neither supreme, how soon confusion
May enter 'twixt the gap of both and take
The one by the other.
    Com.   Well, on to the market place.
    Cor. Whoever gave that counsel to give forth   145
The corn o' the storehouse gratis, as 'twas used
Sometime in Greece—
    Men.   Well, well, no more of that.
    Cor. Though there the people had more absolute
        pow'r—   150
I say they nourished disobedience, fed
The ruin of the state.
    Bru.   Why, shall the people give
One that speaks thus their voice?
    Cor.   I'll give my reasons, 155
More worthier than their voices. They know the corn
Was not our recompense, resting well assured
They ne'er did service for't; being pressed to the war,
Even when the navel of the state was touched,
They would not thread the gates. This kind of service 160
Did not deserve corn gratis. Being i' the war,
Their mutinies and revolts, wherein they showed
Most valor, spoke not for them. The accusation
Which they have often made against the Senate,
All cause unborn, could never be the native   165
Of our so frank donation. Well, what then?
How shall this bosom multiplied digest
The Senate's courtesy? Let deeds express

173. **cares:** concerns for the people's welfare.

180. **Seal:** confirm; as at II.[iii.]111; **double worship:** dual rule.

182. **gentry:** gentle birth.

183. **conclude:** decide.

184. **general ignorance:** the ignorant multitude; **omit:** neglect.

186. **unstable slightness:** giddy triviality; **Purpose so barred:** purposeful planning thus prevented.

192. **jump:** jolt.

194. **multitudinous tongue:** tongue of the multitude.

197. **integrity:** singleminded action.

What's like to be their words: "We did request it;
We are the greater poll, and in true fear   170
They gave us our demands." Thus we debase
The nature of our seats, and make the rabble
Call our cares fears; which will in time
Break ope the locks o' the Senate and bring in
The crows to peck the eagles.   175

   Men.   Come, enough.

   Bru. Enough, with over measure.

   Cor.   No, take more.

What may be sworn by, both divine and human,
Seal what I end withal! This double worship,   180
Where one part does disdain with cause, the other
Insult without all reason; where gentry, title, wisdom,
Cannot conclude but by the yea and no
Of general ignorance—it must omit
Real necessities, and give way the while   185
To unstable slightness. Purpose so barred, it follows
Nothing is done to purpose. Therefore, beseech you—
You that will be less fearful than discreet;
That love the fundamental part of state
More than you doubt the change on't; that prefer   190
A noble life before a long, and wish
To jump a body with a dangerous physic
That's sure of death without it—at once pluck out
The multitudinous tongue; let them not lick
The sweet which is their poison. Your dishonor   195
Mangles true judgment and bereaves the state
Of that integrity which should become't,
Not having the power to do the good it would,
For the ill which doth control't.

206. **the greater bench:** officials of greater dignity.

209. **Let what is meet be said it must be meet:** i.e., tell the people that they must accept what we consider appropriate action.

213. **ædiles:** magistrates, who during this period were plebeians.

217. **Attach:** arrest.

219. **to thine answer:** to make your defense.

Bru.   Has said enough.   200
Sic. Has spoken like a traitor and shall answer
As traitors do.
Cor.   Thou wretch, despite o'erwhelm thee!
What should the people do with these bald tribunes,
On whom depending, their obedience fails   205
To the greater bench? In a rebellion,
When what's not meet, but what must be, was law,
Then were they chosen; in a better hour
Let what is meet be said it must be meet,
And throw their power i' the dust.   210
Bru. Manifest treason!
Sic.   This a consul? No.
Bru. The ædiles, ho!

Enter an Ædile.

              Let him be apprehended.
Sic. Go call the people, [*Exit Ædile.*] in whose   215
    name myself
Attach thee as a traitorous innovator,
A foe to the public weal. Obey, I charge thee,
And follow to thine answer.
Cor.   Hence, old goat!   220
Pat. We'll surety him.
Com.   Aged sir, hands off.
Cor. Hence, rotten thing! Or I shall shake thy bones
Out of thy garments.
Sic.   Help, ye citizens!   225

242. **at point:** about.

Enter a rabble of Plebeians, with the Ædiles.

Men. On both sides more respect.

Sic. Here's he that would take from you all your
    power.

Bru. Seize him, ædiles.

Pleb. Down with him! Down with him!   230

2. Sen. Weapons, weapons, weapons!
             They all bustle about Coriolanus.

All. Tribunes! Patricians! Citizens! What, ho!
    Sicinius! Brutus! Coriolanus! Citizens!

Pat. Peace, peace, peace; stay, hold, peace!

Men. What is about to be? I am out of breath;   235
Confusion's near; I cannot speak. You tribunes
To the people—Coriolanus, patience!
Speak, good Sicinius.

Sic.   Hear me, people; peace!

Pleb. Let's hear our tribune. Peace! Speak, speak,   240
    speak.

Sic. You are at point to lose your liberties.
Marcius would have all from you; Marcius,
Whom late you have named for consul.

Men.   Fie, fie, fie!   245
This is the way to kindle, not to quench.

1. Sen. To unbuild the city, and to lay all flat.

Sic. What is the city but the people?

Pleb.   True,
The people are the city.   250

Bru. By the consent of all we were established
The people's magistrates.

260. **Or:** either.

266. **the rock Tarpeian:** a rock face on the Capitoline Hill, from which criminals were pushed to their deaths.

Pleb.   You so remain.

Men. And so are like to do.

Com. That is the way to lay the city flat,   255
To bring the roof to the foundation,
And bury all which yet distinctly ranges
In heaps and piles of ruin.

Sic.   This deserves death.

Bru. Or let us stand to our authority   260
Or let us lose it. We do here pronounce,
Upon the part o' the people, in whose power
We were elected theirs, Marcius is worthy
Of present death.

Sic.   Therefore lay hold of him;   265
Bear him to the rock Tarpeian, and from thence
Into destruction cast him.

Bru.   Ædiles, seize him.

Pleb. Yield, Marcius, yield.

Men. Hear me one word; beseech you, tribunes,   270
Hear me but a word.

Æd. Peace, peace!

Men. Be that you seem, truly your country's friend,
And temp'rately proceed to what you would
Thus violently redress.   275

Bru.   Sir, those cold ways,
That seem like prudent helps, are very poisonous
Where the disease is violent. Lay hands upon him
And bear him to the rock.

                  Coriolanus draws his sword.

Cor.   No: I'll die here.   280
There's some among you have beheld me fighting;
Come, try upon yourselves what you have seen me.

299. **tent:** treat; see I.[ix.]36.

306. **One time will owe another:** i.e., a better time will come.

Men. Down with that sword! Tribunes, withdraw
  awhile.

Bru. Lay hands upon him. 285

Men.   Help Marcius, help,
You that be noble; help him, young and old.

Pleb. Down with him, down with him!

*In this mutiny the Tribunes, the Ædiles, and the
                        people are beat in.*

Men. Go, get you to your house; be gone, away.
All will be nought else. 290

2. Sen.   Get you gone.

Cor.   Stand fast;
We have as many friends as enemies.

Men. Shall it be put to that?

1. Sen.   The gods forbid! 295
I prithee, noble friend, home to thy house;
Leave us to cure this cause.

Men.   For 'tis a sore upon us
You cannot tent yourself; be gone, beseech you.

Com. Come, sir, along with us. 300

Cor. I would they were barbarians, as they are,
Though in Rome littered; not Romans, as they are not,
Though calved i' the porch o' the Capitol.

Men.   Be gone.
Put not your worthy rage into your tongue; 305
One time will owe another.

Cor.   On fair ground
I could beat forty of them.

Men.   I could myself
Take up a brace o' the best of them; yea, the two trib- 310
  unes.

315. tag: rag, tag, and bobtail; rabble.

Neptune. From Guillaume Du Choul, *Discours de la religion des anciens Romains* (1581).

Com. But now 'tis odds beyond arithmetic,
And manhood is called foolery when it stands
Against a falling fabric. Will you hence,
Before the tag return? whose rage doth rend   315
Like interrupted waters, and o'erbear
What they are used to bear.

Men.   Pray you be gone.
I'll try whether my old wit be in request
With those that have but little; this must be patched 320
With cloth of any color.

Com.   Nay, come away.
    Exeunt Coriolanus and Cominius, [with others].

Pat. This man has marred his fortune.

Men. His nature is too noble for the world:
He would not flatter Neptune for his trident,   325
Or Jove for's power to thunder. His heart's his mouth;
What his breast forges, that his tongue must vent;
And, being angry, does forget that ever
He heard the name of death.   *A noise within.*
Here's goodly work!   330

Pat.   I would they were a-bed.

Men. I would they were in Tiber.
What the vengeance, could he not speak 'em fair?

Enter Brutus and Sicinius, with the rabble again.

Sic. Where is this viper
That would depopulate the city and   335
Be every man himself?

Men.   You worthy tribunes—

Sic. He shall be thrown down the Tarpeian rock

349. **cry havoc:** call for merciless slaughter. The cry of **havoc** was the signal for "no quarter."

352. **holp:** helped.

366. **peremptory:** resolute.

With rigorous hands; he hath resisted law,
And therefore law shall scorn him further trial   340
Than the severity of the public power,
Which he so sets at nought.

1. Cit.   He shall well know
The noble tribunes are the people's mouths,
And we their hands.   345

Pleb.   He shall, sure on't.

Men.   Sir, sir—

Sic. Peace!

Men. Do not cry havoc, where you should but hunt
With modest warrant.   350

Sic.   Sir, how comes't that you
Have holp to make this rescue?

Men.   Hear me speak.
As I do know the consul's worthiness,
So can I name his faults.   355

Sic.   Consul! What consul?

Men. The consul Coriolanus.

Bru.   He consul!

Pleb. No, no, no, no, no.

Men. If, by the tribunes' leave, and yours, good 360
    people,
I may be heard, I would crave a word or two;
The which shall turn you to no further harm
Than so much loss of time.

Sic.   Speak briefly, then,   365
For we are peremptory to dispatch
This viperous traitor; to eject him hence
Were but one danger, and to keep him here

386. **clean kam:** quite askew.
387. **Merely:** absolutely.
399. **process:** due legal form.

Our certain death; therefore it is decreed
He dies tonight.   370
   Men.   Now the good gods forbid
That our renowned Rome, whose gratitude
Towards her deserved children is enrolled
In Jove's own book, like an unnatural dam
Should now eat up her own!   375
   Sic. He's a disease that must be cut away.
   Men. O, he's a limb that has but a disease:
Mortal to cut it off; to cure it easy.
What has he done to Rome that's worthy death?
Killing our enemies, the blood he hath lost—   380
Which I dare vouch is more than that he hath
By many an ounce—he dropped it for his country;
And what is left, to lose it by his country
Were to us all that do't and suffer it
A brand to the end o' the world.   385
   Sic.   This is clean kam.
   Bru. Merely awry. When he did love his country,
It honored him.
   Sic.   The service of the foot,
Being once gangrened, is not then respected   390
For what before it was.
   Bru.   We'll hear no more.
Pursue him to his house and pluck him thence,
Lest his infection, being of catching nature,
Spread further.   395
   Men.   One word more, one word:
This tiger-footed rage, when it shall find
The harm of unscanned swiftness, will, too late,
Tie leaden pounds to's heels. Proceed by process,

408. bolted: sifted; selected.

Lest parties—as he is beloved—break out,   400
And sack great Rome with Romans.
   Bru.   If it were so—
   Sic. What do ye talk?
Have we not had a taste of his obedience—
Our ædiles smote, ourselves resisted? Come!   405
   Men. Consider this: he has been bred i' the wars
Since 'a could draw a sword, and is ill schooled
In bolted language; meal and bran together
He throws without distinction. Give me leave,
I'll go to him and undertake to bring him   410
Where he shall answer by a lawful form,
In peace, to his utmost peril.
   1. Sen.   Noble tribunes,
It is the humane way; the other course
Will prove too bloody, and the end of it   415
Unknown to the beginning.
   Sic.   Noble Menenius,
Be you then as the people's officer.
Masters, lay down your weapons.
   Bru.   Go not home.   420
   Sic. Meet on the market place. We'll attend you
     there;
Where, if you bring not Marcius, we'll proceed
In our first way.
   Men.   I'll bring him to you.   425
[*To the Senators*] Let me desire your company; he
     must come,
Or what is worst will follow.
   1. Sen.   Pray you let's to him.
                               Exeunt.

III. [**ii.**] 8. **muse:** wonder.
10. **woolen:** i.e., woolen-clad.
13. **ordinance:** rank.

[Scene II. The same. A room in Coriolanus' house.]

Enter Coriolanus with Nobles.

Cor. Let them pull all about mine ears, present me
Death on the wheel or at wild horses' heels;
Or pile ten hills on the Tarpeian rock,
That the precipitation might down stretch
Below the beam of sight; yet will I still   5
Be thus to them.
    1. Pat.   You do the nobler.
    Cor. I muse my mother
Does not approve me further, who was wont
To call them woolen vassals, things created   10
To buy and sell with groats; to show bare heads
In congregations, to yawn, be still, and wonder,
When one but of my ordinance stood up
To speak of peace or war.

Enter Volumnia.

                          I talk of you: 15
Why did you wish me milder? Would you have me
False to my nature? Rather say I play
The man I am.
    Vol.   O, sir, sir, sir,
I would have had you put your power well on   20
Before you had worn it out.
    Cor.   Let go.
    Vol. You might have been enough the man you are

25. **thwartings:** Theobald's reading; the Folio has "things"; **dispositions:** tempers; specifically, his attitude toward the people.

27. **Ere they lacked power:** before they lost the power. Once Coriolanus had been invested as consul, in other words, it would have been safer to express his unpopular opinions.

34-5. **Unless:** unless Coriolanus does as they ask, the city will **Cleave,** etc.

37. **apt:** yielding; flexible.

41. **herd:** Warburton's reading; the Folio has "heart."

51. **absolute:** inflexible.

With striving less to be so; lesser had been
The thwartings of your dispositions if   25
You had not showed them how ye were disposed,
Ere they lacked power to cross you.

 Cor. Let them hang.

 Vol.   Ay, and burn too.

    Enter Menenius with the Senators.

 Men. Come, come, you have been too rough, some-   30
  thing too rough;
You must return and mend it.

 1. Sen.   There's no remedy,
Unless, by not so doing, our good city
Cleave in the midst and perish.   35

 Vol.   Pray be counseled;
I have a heart as little apt as yours,
But yet a brain that leads my use of anger
To better vantage.

 Men. Well said, noble woman!   40
Before he should thus stoop to the herd, but that
The violent fit o' the time craves it as physic
For the whole state, I would put mine armor on,
Which I can scarcely bear.

 Cor.   What must I do?   45

 Men. Return to the tribunes.

 Cor.   Well, what then, what then?

 Men. Repent what you have spoke.

 Cor. For them! I cannot do it to the gods;
Must I then do't to them?   50

 Vol.   You are too absolute;

53. **extremities speak:** emergency requires.

54. **policy:** politic behavior; circumspection.

65. **stands in like request:** is similarly needed.

66. **force:** emphasize.

70-1. **roted in/Your tongue:** some editors read "rooted"; the Folio spells "roated." In any case, the meaning is that the words come off his tongue but do not proceed from his heart.

72. **Of no allowance to:** without acknowledgment by.

79. **I am:** I represent; speak for.

Though therein you can never be too noble
But when extremities speak. I have heard you say
Honor and policy, like unsevered friends,
I' the war do grow together; grant that, and tell me   55
In peace what each of them by the other lose
That they combine not there.

 Cor.   Tush, tush!

 Men.   A good demand.

 Vol. If it be honor in your wars to seem   60
The same you are not, which for your best ends
You adopt your policy, how is it less or worse
That it shall hold companionship in peace
With honor as in war; since that to both
It stands in like request?   65

 Cor.   Why force you this?

 Vol. Because that now it lies you on to speak
To the people, not by your own instruction,
Nor by the matter which your heart prompts you,
But with such words that are but roted in   70
Your tongue, though but bastards and syllables
Of no allowance to your bosom's truth.
Now, this no more dishonors you at all
Than to take in a town with gentle words,
Which else would put you to your fortune and   75
The hazard of much blood.
I would dissemble with my nature where
My fortunes and my friends at stake required
I should do so in honor. I am in this
Your wife, your son, these senators, the nobles;   80
And you will rather show our general louts

83. **inheritance:** possession.

86. **salve:** smooth over.

87-8. **Not what is dangerous present, but the loss/Of what is past:** not only the danger present but the loss of the consulship.

91. **here be with them:** i.e., get around them in this way; get home to them by the following humble actions.

92. **bussing:** kissing.

94. **waving:** bowing.

95. **Which often:** which do often.

How you can frown than spend a fawn upon 'em
For the inheritance of their loves and safeguard
Of what that want might ruin.

   Men.   Noble lady!   85
Come, go with us, speak fair; you may salve so,
Not what is dangerous present, but the loss
Of what is past.

   Vol.   I prithee now, my son,
Go to them with this bonnet in thy hand;   90
And thus far having stretched it, here be with them,
Thy knee bussing the stones—for in such business
Action is eloquence, and the eyes of the ignorant
More learned than the ears—waving thy head,
Which often, thus correcting thy stout heart,   95
Now humble as the ripest mulberry
That will not hold the handling. Or say to them
Thou art their soldier and, being bred in broils,
Hast not the soft way which, thou dost confess,
Were fit for thee to use as they to claim,   100
In asking their good loves; but thou wilt frame
Thyself, forsooth, hereafter theirs, so far
As thou hast power and person.

   Men.   This but done
Even as she speaks, why, their hearts were yours; 105
For they have pardons, being asked, as free
As words to little purpose.

   Vol.   Prithee now,
Go, and be ruled; although I know thou hadst rather
Follow thine enemy in a fiery gulf   110
Than flatter him in a bower.

121. **unbarbed sconce:** unhelmeted head.

125-26. **single plot . . ./mold:** single piece of earth; single human body.

137. **harlot:** base creature, a word used to describe both men and women, not invariably wantons.

138. **Which quired with my drum:** which formerly sounded in harmony with my drum.

Enter Cominius.

        Here is Cominius.
 Com. I have been i' the market place; and, sir, 'tis fit
You make strong party, or defend yourself
By calmness or by absence; all's in anger.   115
 Men. Only fair speech.
 Com.   I think 'twill serve, if he
Can thereto frame his spirit.
 Vol.   He must and will.
Prithee now, say you will, and go about it.   120
 Cor. Must I go show them my unbarbed sconce?
  Must I
With my base tongue give to my noble heart
A lie that it must bear? Well, I will do't;
Yet, were there but this single plot to lose,   125
This mold of Marcius, they to dust should grind it,
And throw't against the wind. To the market place!
You have put me now to such a part which never
I shall discharge to the life.
 Com.   Come, come, we'll prompt you. 130
 Vol. I prithee now, sweet son, as thou hast said
My praises made thee first a soldier, so,
To have my praise for this, perform a part
Thou hast not done before.
 Cor.   Well, I must do't.   135
Away, my disposition, and possess me
Some harlot's spirit! My throat of war be turned,
Which quired with my drum, into a pipe
Small as an eunuch or the virgin voice

141. **Tent:** lodge.

146. **surcease:** cease.

151-53. **Let/Thy mother rather feel thy pride than fear/Thy dangerous stoutness:** Volumnia is resigned to the fate that Coriolanus' pride and obstinacy are about to bring upon him and the state. She prefers to sympathize with his pride than to fear any longer his obstinacy.

156. **owe:** own.

159. **mountebank their loves:** win their affection with the cheap tricks of a mountebank.

160. **Cog:** swindle.

Consuls addressing troops. From Guillaume Du Choul, *Discours de la religion des anciens Romains* (1581).

That babies lulls asleep! The smiles of knaves   140
Tent in my cheeks, and schoolboys' tears take up
The glasses of my sight! A beggar's tongue
Make motion through my lips, and my armed knees,
Who bowed but in my stirrup, bend like his
That hath received an alms! I will not do't,   145
Lest I surcease to honor mine own truth,
And by my body's action teach my mind
A most inherent baseness.
   Vol.   At thy choice, then.
To beg of thee, it is my more dishonor   150
Than thou of them. Come all to ruin. Let
Thy mother rather feel thy pride than fear
Thy dangerous stoutness; for I mock at death
With as big heart as thou. Do as thou list.
Thy valiantness was mine, thou suckedst it from me; 155
But owe thy pride thyself.
   Cor.   .   Pray be content.
Mother, I am going to the market place;
Chide me no more. I'll mountebank their loves,
Cog their hearts from them, and come home beloved 160
Of all the trades in Rome. Look, I am going.
Commend me to my wife. I'll return consul,
Or never trust to what my tongue can do
I' the way of flattery further.
   Vol.   Do your will.   *Exit.* 165
   Com. Away! The tribunes do attend you. Arm your-
     self
To answer mildly; for they are prepared
With accusations, as I hear, more strong
Than are upon you yet.   170

III. [iii.] 1. **home:** emphatically. See **home** at I. [iv.] 49 and II. [ii.] 116.

3. **Enforce him:** press hard upon.

17. **presently:** at once.

Cor. The word is "mildly." Pray you let us go.
Let them accuse me by invention; I
Will answer in mine honor.
    Men.   Ay, but mildly.
    Cor. Well, mildly be it then—mildly.   175

                                    Exeunt.

[Scene III. The same. The Forum.]

Enter Sicinius and Brutus.

  Bru. In this point charge him home, that he affects
Tyrannical power. If he evade us there,
Enforce him with his envy to the people,
And that the spoil got on the Antiates
Was ne'er distributed.   5

Enter an Ædile.

                    What, will he come?
  Æd. He's coming.
  Bru.   How accompanied?
  Æd. With old Menenius, and those senators
That always favored him.   10
  Sic.   Have you a catalogue
Of all the voices that we have procured,
Set down by the poll?
  Æd.   I have; 'tis ready.
  Sic. Have you collected them by tribes?   15
  Æd.   I have.
  Sic. Assemble presently the people hither;

30. **hint:** opportunity.

33. **Put him to choler straight:** arouse his anger immediately.

34-5. **have his worth/Of contradiction:** indulge his contrariness to the full.

41. **ostler:** groom.

42. **bear the knave by the volume:** stand being called a knave to the very limit.

And when they hear me say, "It shall be so
I' the right and strength o' the commons," be it either
For death, for fine, or banishment, then let them,   20
If I say fine, cry "Fine!"—if death, cry "Death!"
Insisting on the old prerogative
And power i' the truth o' the cause.

    Æd.   I shall inform them.

    Bru. And when such time they have begun to cry,   25
Let them not cease, but with a din confused
Enforce the present execution
Of what we chance to sentence.

    Æd.   Very well.

    Sic. Make them be strong and ready for this hint,   30
When we shall hap to give't them.

    Bru.   Go about it.
                        [*Exit Ædile.*]
Put him to choler straight. He hath been used
Ever to conquer, and to have his worth
Of contradiction; being once chafed, he cannot   35
Be reined again to temperance; then he speaks
What's in his heart, and that is there which looks
With us to break his neck.

*Enter Coriolanus, Menenius, and Cominius, with
                 others.*

    Sic.   Well, here he comes.

    Men. Calmly, I do beseech you.   40

    Cor. Ay, as an ostler, that for the poorest piece
Will bear the knave by the volume. The honored gods
Keep Rome in safety, and the chairs of justice

55. determine: be settled.
58. Allow: acknowledge.

Supplied with worthy men! Plant love among's!
Throng our large temples with the shows of peace, 45
And not our streets with war!
  1. Sen.   Amen, amen!
  Men. A noble wish.

    [Re-]*enter the Ædile, with the Plebeians.*

  Sic. Draw near, ye people.
  Æd. List to your tribunes. Audience! Peace, I say! 50
  Cor. First, hear me speak.
  Both Trib.   Well, say. Peace, ho!
  Cor. Shall I be charged no further than this pres-
    ent?
Must all determine here?   55
  Sic.   I do demand,
If you submit you to the people's voices,
Allow their officers, and are content
To suffer lawful censure for such faults
As shall be proved upon you.   60
  Cor.   I am content.
  Men. Lo, citizens, he says he is content.
The warlike service he has done, consider; think
Upon the wounds his body bears, which show
Like graves i' the holy churchyard.   65
  Cor.   Scratches with briers,
Scars to move laughter only.
  Men.   Consider further,
That when he speaks not like a citizen,
You find him like a soldier; do not take   70

73. **envy you:** i.e., such sounds as express malice against you.

82. **seasoned office:** equitable division of the government, allowing the people their representatives.

88. **injurious:** insulting.

His rougher accents for malicious sounds,
But, as I say, such as become a soldier
Rather than envy you.
   Com.   Well, well! No more.
   Cor. What is the matter,   75
That being passed for consul with full voice,
I am so dishonored that the very hour
You take it off again?
   Sic.   Answer to us.
   Cor. Say then; 'tis true, I ought so.   80
   Sic. We charge you that you have contrived to take
From Rome all seasoned office, and to wind
Yourself into a power tyrannical;
For which you are a traitor to the people.
   Cor. How! Traitor!   85
   Men.   Nay, temperately! Your promise.
   Cor. The fires i' the lowest hell fold in the people!
Call me their traitor! Thou injurious tribune!
Within thine eyes sat twenty thousand deaths,
In thy hands clutched as many millions, in   90
Thy lying tongue both numbers, I would say
"Thou liest" unto thee with a voice as free
As I do pray the gods.
   Sic.   Mark you this, people?
   Pleb. To the rock, to the rock with him!   95
   Sic. Peace!
We need not put new matter to his charge.
What you have seen him do and heard him speak,
Beating your officers, cursing yourselves,
Opposing laws with strokes, and here defying   100

114. **pent:** confined.
119. **For that:** because.

Those whose great power must try him—even this,
So criminal and in such capital kind,
Deserves the extremest death.
 Bru.   But since he hath
Served well for Rome—   105
 Cor.   What do you prate of service?
 Bru. I talk of that that know it.
 Cor.   You!
 Men. Is this the promise that you made your
  mother?   110
 Com. Know, I pray you—
 Cor.   I'll know no further.
Let them pronounce the steep Tarpeian death,
Vagabond exile, flaying, pent to linger
But with a grain a day, I would not buy   115
Their mercy at the price of one fair word,
Nor check my courage for what they can give,
To have't with saying, "Good morrow."
 Sic. For that he has,
As much as in him lies, from time to time   120
Envied against the people, seeking means
To pluck away their power; as now at last
Given hostile strokes, and that not in the presence
Of dreaded justice, but on the ministers
That do distribute it—in the name o' the people, 125
And in the power of us the tribunes, we,
Ev'n from this instant, banish him our city,
In peril of precipitation
From off the rock Tarpeian, never more
To enter our Rome gates. I' the people's name, 130

142. **estimate:** reputation.
150. **cry:** pack.

I say it shall be so.

   Pleb. It shall be so, it shall be so! Let him away!
He's banished, and it shall be so.

   Com. Hear me, my masters and my common
     friends—   135

   Sic. He's sentenced; no more hearing.

   Com.   Let me speak.
I have been consul, and can show for Rome
Her enemies' marks upon me. I do love
My country's good with a respect more tender,   140
More holy and profound, than mine own life,
My dear wife's estimate, her womb's increase
And treasure of my loins. Then if I would
Speak that—

   Sic.   We know your drift. Speak what?   145

   Bru. There's no more to be said, but he is banished,
As enemy to the people and his country.
It shall be so.

   Pleb.   It shall be so, it shall be so.

   Cor. You common cry of curs, whose breath I hate 150
As reek o' the rotten fens, whose loves I prize
As the dead carcasses of unburied men
That do corrupt my air—I banish you.
And here remain with your uncertainty!
Let every feeble rumor shake your hearts;   155
Your enemies, with nodding of their plumes,
Fan you into despair! Have the power still
To banish your defenders, till at length
Your ignorance, which finds not till it feels,
Making but reservation of yourselves   160
Still your own foes, deliver you

162. **abated:** dispirited and humbled.
167. **Hoo-oo:** hurrah.

As most abated captives to some nation
That won you without blows! Despising
For you the city, thus I turn my back;
There is a world elsewhere. *Exeunt Coriolanus,* 165
  Cominius, Menenius, [with the other Patricians].
 Æd. The people's enemy is gone, is gone!
    They all shout and throw up their caps.
 Pleb. Our enemy is banished, he is gone! Hoo-oo!
 Sic. Go see him out at gates, and follow him,
As he hath followed you, with all despite;
Give him deserved vexation. Let a guard   170
Attend us through the city.
 Pleb. Come, come, let's see him out at gates; come!
The gods preserve our noble tribunes! Come.
          Exeunt.

THE TRAGEDY OF
CORIOLANUS

ACT IV

IV. Saying farewell to his wife, mother, and friends at the gates of Rome, Coriolanus is strangely resigned and voices the belief that he will be missed.

Coriolanus, however, visits his old enemy, Tullus Aufidius, at Antium, and places his life in his hands. He will either help Aufidius conquer Rome or Aufidius can put him to death. Aufidius receives him generously and appoints him commander of the Volscian troops in a new assault on Rome.

Brutus and Sicinius are congratulating themselves for bringing about Coriolanus' exile when word is received that he is leading the Volsces against the city. Cominius and Menenius reproach the tribunes for having contrived Rome's destruction.

Aufidius, always jealous of Coriolanus, is soon chafing at being in a subordinate position to him, but he foresees that Coriolanus may yet bring about his own destruction.

∎∎∎∎∎∎∎∎∎∎∎∎∎∎∎∎∎∎∎∎∎∎∎∎∎∎

IV.[i.] 8-10. fortune's blows,/When most struck home, being gentle wounded craves/A noble cunning: i.e., when fortune's blows have hit with their full force a true schooling in nobility is necessary for one to endure the wounds without protest.

12. conned: learned.

ACT IV

[Scene I. Rome. Before a gate of the city.]

*Enter Coriolanus, Volumnia, Virgilia, Menenius,
Cominius, with the young Nobility of Rome.*

Cor. Come, leave your tears; a brief farewell. The
    beast
With many heads butts me away. Nay, mother,
Where is your ancient courage? You were used
To say extremities was the trier of spirits;   5
That common chances common men could bear;
That when the sea was calm all boats alike
Showed mastership in floating; fortune's blows,
When most struck home, being gentle wounded craves
A noble cunning. You were used to load me   10
With precepts that would make invincible
The heart that conned them.
   Vir. O heavens! O heavens!
   Cor.   Nay, I prithee, woman—
   Vol. Now the red pestilence strike all trades in 15
    Rome,
And occupations perish!
   Cor.   What, what, what!

30. **fond:** foolish.
31. **wot:** know.
33. **Believe't not lightly:** i.e., be certain of this.
37. **cautelous:** crafty; **practice:** trickery.
41. **exposure:** exposure.
47. **repeal:** recall.

A consul. From Cesare Vecellio, *De gli habiti antichi et moderni* (1590).

I shall be loved when I am lacked. Nay, mother,
Resume that spirit when you were wont to say,   20
If you had been the wife of Hercules,
Six of his labors you'd have done, and saved
Your husband so much sweat. Cominius,
Droop not; adieu. Farewell, my wife, my mother.
I'll do well yet. Thou old and true Menenius,   25
Thy tears are salter than a younger man's
And venomous to thine eyes. My sometime General,
I have seen thee stern, and thou hast oft beheld
Heart-hard'ning spectacles; tell these sad women
'Tis fond to wail inevitable strokes,   30
As 'tis to laugh at 'em. My mother, you wot well
My hazards still have been your solace; and
Believe't not lightly, though I go alone,
Like to a lonely dragon, that his fen
Makes feared and talked of more than seen, your son   35
Will or exceed the common or be caught
With cautelous baits and practice.
   Vol.   My first son,
Whither wilt thou go? Take good Cominius
With thee awhile; determine on some course   40
More than a wild exposture to each chance
That starts i' the way before thee.
   Vir.   O the gods!
   Com. I'll follow thee a month, devise with thee
Where thou shalt rest, that thou mayst hear of us,   45
And we of thee; so, if the time thrust forth
A cause for thy repeal, we shall not send
O'er the vast world to seek a single man,

49. **advantage:** opportunity.
54. **bring:** escort.
56. **noble touch:** tried and true nobility.

And lose advantage, which doth ever cool
I' the absence of the needer.   50
 Cor.   Fare ye well;
Thou hast years upon thee, and thou art too full
Of the wars' surfeits to go rove with one
That's yet unbruised; bring me but out at gate.
Come, my sweet wife, my dearest mother, and   55
My friends of noble touch; when I am forth,
Bid me farewell, and smile. I pray you come.
While I remain above the ground you shall
Hear from me still, and never of me aught
But what is like me formerly.   60
 Men.   That's worthily
As any ear can hear. Come, let's not weep.
If I could shake off but one seven years
From these old arms and legs, by the good gods,
I'd with thee every foot.   65
 Cor.   Give me thy hand.
Come.

           Exeunt.

[Scene II. The same. A street near the gate.]

*Enter the two Tribunes, Sicinius and Brutus,
with the Ædile.*

 Sic. Bid them all home; he's gone, and we'll no fur-
  ther.
The nobility are vexed, whom we see have sided
In his behalf.
 Bru. Now we have shown our power,   5

IV. [ii.] 27. mankind: Sicinius asks insultingly if she is a mannish woman, a virago, and Volumnia replies as if she understood him to ask whether she was of the human race.

29. Hadst thou foxship: was it because you were a fox.

A tribune. From Guillaume Du Choul, *Discours de la religion des anciens Romains* (1581).

Let us seem humbler after it is done
Than when it was a-doing.
   Sic.   Bid them home.
Say their great enemy is gone, and they
Stand in their ancient strength.   10
   Bru.   Dismiss them home.
                          Exit Ædile.
Here comes his mother.

     Enter Volumnia, Virgilia, and Menenius.

   Sic.   Let's not meet her.
   Bru.   Why?
   Sic. They say she's mad.   15
   Bru. They have ta'en note of us; keep on your way.
   Vol. O, y'are well met; the hoarded plague o' the
    gods
Requite your love!
   Men.   Peace, peace, be not so loud.   20
   Vol. If that I could for weeping, you should hear—
Nay, and you shall hear some. [*To Brutus*] Will you
    be gone?
   Vir. [*To Sicinius*] You shall stay too. I would I had
    the power   25
To say so to my husband.
   Sic.   Are you mankind?
   Vol. Ay, fool; is that a shame? Note but this, fool:
Was not a man my father? Hadst thou foxship
To banish him that struck more blows for Rome   30
Than thou hast spoken words?
   Sic.   O blessed heavens!

36. **in Arabia:** i.e., where you would be defenseless and at his mercy; **tribe:** family.

55. **brave:** noble.

   Vol. Mo noble blows than ever thou wise words;
And for Rome's good. I'll tell thee what—yet go!
Nay, but thou shalt stay too. I would my son   35
Were in Arabia, and thy tribe before him,
His good sword in his hand.
   Sic.   What then?
   Vir.   What then!
He'd make an end of thy posterity.   40
   Vol. Bastards and all.
Good man, the wounds that he does bear for Rome!
   Men. Come, come, peace.
   Sic. I would he had continued to his country
As he began, and not unknit himself   45
The noble knot he made.
   Bru.   I would he had.
   Vol. "I would he had!" 'Twas you incensed the
      rabble—
Cats that can judge as fitly of his worth   50
As I can of those mysteries which heaven
Will not have earth to know.
   Bru.   Pray, let's go.
   Vol. Now, pray, sir, get you gone:
You have done a brave deed. Ere you go, hear this: 55
As far as doth the Capitol exceed
The meanest house in Rome, so far my son—
This lady's husband here, this, do you see?—
Whom you have banished does exceed you all.
   Bru. Well, well, we'll leave you.   60
   Sic.   Why stay we to be baited
With one that wants her wits?   *Exeunt Tribunes.*
   Vol.   Take my prayers with you.

72. **faint puling:** weak whimpering.

||||||||||||||||||||||||||||||||||||||||||||||||||||||||

IV.[iii.]9. your favor is well appeared by your tongue: your identity is proclaimed by your speech. **Favor** means facial appearance.

I would the gods had nothing else to do
But to confirm my curses. Could I meet 'em   65
But once a day, it would unclog my heart
Of what lies heavy to't.

Men.   You have told them home,
And, by my troth, you have cause. You'll sup with me?

Vol. Anger's my meat; I sup upon myself,   70
And so shall starve with feeding. Come, let's go.
Leave this faint puling and lament as I do,
In anger, Juno-like. Come, come, come.

> *Exeunt [Volumnia and Virgilia].*

Men. Fie, fie, fie!   [*Exit.*]

|||||||||||||||||||||||||||||||||||||||||||||||||||||||||||||||||||||||||||||||||||

[Scene III. A highway between Rome and Antium.]

Enter a Roman and a Volsce, [meeting].

Rom. I know you well, sir, and you know me; your
name, I think, is Adrian.

Vols. It is so, sir. Truly, I have forgot you.

Rom. I am a Roman; and my services are, as you
are, against 'em. Know you me yet?   5

Vols. Nicanor? No!

Rom. The same, sir.

Vols. You had more beard when I last saw you, but
your favor is well appeared by your tongue. What's
the news in Rome? I have a note from the Volscian   10
state to find you out there. You have well saved me a
day's journey.

Rom. There hath been in Rome strange insurrec-

34. **in no request of:** no longer wanted by.
36. **cannot choose:** cannot fail (to appear well).
43-4 **distinctly billeted:** enrolled by companies;
in the entertainment: on the payroll; hired.

tions: the people against the senators, patricians, and
nobles.   15

Vols. Hath been! Is it ended, then? Our state thinks
not so; they are in a most warlike preparation, and
hope to come upon them in the heat of their division.

Rom. The main blaze of it is past, but a small thing
would make it flame again; for the nobles receive so   20
to heart the banishment of that worthy Coriolanus
that they are in a ripe aptness to take all power from
the people and to pluck from them their tribunes forever. This lies glowing, I can tell you, and is almost
mature for the violent breaking out.   25

Vols. Coriolanus banished!

Rom. Banished, sir.

Vols. You will be welcome with this intelligence,
Nicanor.

Rom. The day serves well for them now. I have   30
heard it said the fittest time to corrupt a man's wife is
when she's fall'n out with her husband. Your noble
Tullus Aufidius will appear well in these wars, his
great opposer, Coriolanus, being now in no request of
his country.   35

Vols. He cannot choose. I am most fortunate thus
accidentally to encounter you; you have ended my
business, and I will merrily accompany you home.

Rom. I shall between this and supper tell you most
strange things from Rome, all tending to the good of   40
their adversaries. Have you an army ready, say you?

Vols. A most royal one: the centurions and their
charges, distinctly billeted, already in the entertainment, and to be on foot at an hour's warning.

Rom. I am joyful to hear of their readiness, and am　45
the man, I think, that shall set them in present action.
So, sir, heartily well met, and most glad of your
company.

Vols. You take my part from me, sir. I have the
most cause to be glad of yours.　50

Rom. Well, let us go together.

　　　　　　　　　　　　　　　　　　Exeunt.

[Scene IV. Antium. Before Aufidius' house.]

Enter Coriolanus, in mean apparel, disguised and
muffled.

　Cor. A goodly city is this Antium. City,
'Tis I that made thy widows: many an heir
Of these fair edifices fore my wars
Have I heard groan and drop. Then know me not,
Lest that thy wives with spits and boys with stones,　5
In puny battle slay me.

　　　　　　　　Enter a Citizen.

　　　　　　　　Save you, sir.
　Cit. And you.
　Cor. Direct me, if it be your will,
Where great Aufidius lies. Is he in Antium?　10
　Cit. He is, and feasts the nobles of the state
At his house this night.
　Cor.　　　　　　Which is his house, beseech you?
　Cit. This here before you.

IV. [iv.] 21. **On a dissension of a doit:** over a trivial difference; see **doit** at I. [v.] 6.

22. **fellest:** deadliest.

25. **trick:** toy; trifle.

26. **interjoin their issues:** make common cause.

29. **way:** admittance.

Cor.   Thank you, sir; farewell.   15
                                    Exit Citizen.

O world, thy slippery turns! Friends now fast sworn,
Whose double bosoms seems to wear one heart,
Whose hours, whose bed, whose meal and exercise
Are still together, who twin, as 'twere, in love
Unseparable, shall within this hour,   20
On a dissension of a doit, break out
To bitterest enmity; so fellest foes,
Whose passions and whose plots have broke their sleep
To take the one the other, by some chance,
Some trick not worth an egg, shall grow dear friends   25
And interjoin their issues. So with me:
My birthplace hate I, and my love's upon
This enemy town. I'll enter. If he slay me,
He does fair justice: if he give me way,
I'll do his country service.   30
                                    Exit.

[Scene V. The same. A hall in Aufidius' house.]

Music plays. Enter a Servingman.

1. Ser. Wine, wine, wine! What service is here! I
think our fellows are asleep.   [*Exit.*]

Enter another Servingman.

2. Ser. Where's Cotus? My master calls for him.
Cotus!   [*Exit.*]

IV. [v.] 10. **entertainment:** reception.
13-4. **companions:** base fellows.

Enter Coriolanus.

Cor. A goodly house. The feast smells well, but I 5
Appear not like a guest.

[Re-]enter the first Servingman.

1. Ser. What would you have, friend?
Whence are you? Here's no place for you: pray go to
  the door.   *[Exit.]*
 Cor. I have deserved no better entertainment 10
In being Coriolanus.

[Re-]enter second Servingman.

2. Ser. Whence are you, sir? Has the porter his eyes
in his head that he gives entrance to such companions? Pray get you out.
 Cor. Away!   15
 2. Ser. Away? Get you away.
 Cor. Now th' art troublesome.
 2. Ser. Are you so brave? I'll have you talked with
anon.

Enter a third Servingman. The first meets him.

3. Ser. What fellow's this?   20
 1. Ser. A strange one as ever I looked on. I cannot

25. **avoid:** vacate.
34. **batten:** glut yourself.
46. **daws:** jackdaws.
47. **serve not thy master:** i.e., I am not one of you.

get him out o' the house. Prithee call my master to
him.

3. Ser. What have you to do here, fellow? Pray you
avoid the house.   25

Cor. Let me but stand; I will not hurt your hearth.

3. Ser. What are you?

Cor. A gentleman.

3. Ser. A marv'lous poor one.

Cor. True, so I am.   30

3. Ser. Pray you, poor gentleman, take up some
other station; here's no place for you. Pray you avoid.
Come.

Cor. Follow your function, go and batten on cold
bits.   *Pushes him away from him.* 35

3. Ser. What, you will not? Prithee tell my master
what a strange guest he has here.

2 Ser. And I shall.   *Exit.*

3. Ser. Where dwellst thou?

Cor. Under the canopy.   40

3. Ser. Under the canopy?

Cor. Ay.

3. Ser. Where's that?

Cor. I' the city of kites and crows.

3. Ser. I' the city of kites and crows!   45
What an ass it is! Then thou dwellst with daws too?

Cor. No, I serve not thy master.

3. Ser. How, sir! Do you meddle with my master?

Cor. Ay; 'tis an honester service than to meddle
with thy mistress. Thou pratest and pratest; serve   50
with thy trencher; hence!   *Beats him away.*

68. showst: appearest.

Enter Aufidius with the [second] Servingman.

Auf. Where is this fellow?

2. Ser. Here, sir; I'd have beaten him like a dog but
for disturbing the lords within.

Auf. Whence comest thou? What wouldst thou?   55
    Thy name?
Why speakst not? Speak, man. What's thy name?

Cor. [*Unmuffling*] If, Tullus,
Not yet thou knowst me, and, seeing me, dost not
Think me for the man I am, necessity   60
Commands me name myself.

Auf.   What is thy name?

Cor. A name unmusical to the Volscians' ears,
And harsh in sound to thine.

Auf.   Say, what's thy name?   65
Thou hast a grim appearance, and thy face
Bears a command in't; though thy tackle's torn,
Thou showst a noble vessel. What's thy name?

Cor. Prepare thy brow to frown—knowst thou me
    yet?   70

Auf. I know thee not. Thy name?

Cor. My name is Caius Marcius, who hath done
To thee particularly, and to all the Volsces,
Great hurt and mischief; thereto witness may
My surname, Coriolanus. The painful service,   75
The extreme dangers, and the drops of blood
Shed for my thankless country, are requited
But with that surname—a good memory
And witness of the malice and displeasure

91. **full quit of:** fully revenged on.

93. **heart of wreak:** vengeful heart.

94-5. **particular:** personal; **maims/Of shame:** probably, losses of territory to the Romans.

99. **cank'red:** spiteful; **spleen:** rage.

101. **prove:** attempt.

Which thou shouldst bear me. Only that name re-   80
    mains;
The cruelty and envy of the people,
Permitted by our dastard nobles, who
Have all forsook me, hath devoured the rest,
And suffered me by the voice of slaves to be   85
Whooped out of Rome. Now this extremity
Hath brought me to thy hearth; not out of hope,
Mistake me not, to save my life; for if
I had feared death, of all the men i' the world
I would have 'voided thee; but in mere spite,   90
To be full quit of those my banishers,
Stand I before thee here. Then if thou hast
A heart of wreak in thee, that wilt revenge
Thine own particular wrongs and stop those maims
Of shame seen through thy country, speed thee straight   95
And make my misery serve thy turn. So use it
That my revengeful services may prove
As benefits to thee; for I will fight
Against my cank'red country with the spleen
Of all the under fiends. But if so be   100
Thou darest not this, and that to prove more fortunes
Th'art tired, then, in a word, I also am
Longer to live most weary, and present
My throat to thee and to thy ancient malice;
Which not to cut would show thee but a fool,   105
Since I have ever followed thee with hate,
Drawn tuns of blood out of thy country's breast,
And cannot live but to thy shame, unless
It be to do thee service.
   Auf.   O Marcius, Marcius!   110

118. **grained ash:** ashen spear.

119. **clip:** embrace.

120. **The anvil of my sword:** the object against which I have so often beat my sword—Coriolanus.

129. **power on foot:** army afield.

130. **target:** shield.

The temple of Jupiter in Rome. From Guillaume Du Choul, *Discours de la religion des anciens Romains* (1581).

Each word thou hast spoke hath weeded from my
    heart
A root of ancient envy. If Jupiter
Should from yond cloud speak divine things,
And say, "'Tis true," I'd not believe them more   115
Than thee, all noble Marcius. Let me twine
Mine arms about that body, where against
My grainèd ash an hundred times hath broke
And scarred the moon with splinters; here I clip
The anvil of my sword, and do contest   120
As hotly and as nobly with thy love
As ever in ambitious strength I did
Contend against thy valor. Know thou first,
I loved the maid I married; never man
Sighed truer breath; but that I see thee here,   125
Thou noble thing, more dances my rapt heart
Than when I first my wedded mistress saw
Bestride my threshold. Why, thou Mars, I tell thee
We have a power on foot, and I had purpose
Once more to hew thy target from thy brawn,   130
Or lose mine arm for't. Thou hast beat me out
Twelve several times, and I have nightly since
Dreamt of encounters 'twixt thyself and me—
We have been down together in my sleep,
Unbuckling helms, fisting each other's throat—   135
And waked half dead with nothing. Worthy Marcius,
Had we no other quarrel else to Rome but that
Thou art thence banished, we would muster all
From twelve to seventy, and, pouring war
Into the bowels of ungrateful Rome,   140
Like a bold flood o'erbeat. O, come; go in,

147. **absolute:** perfect.
162. **my mind gave me:** I suspected.

And take our friendly senators by the hands,
Who now are here, taking their leaves of me
Who am prepared against your territories,
Though not for Rome itself.   145
  Cor.   You bless me, gods!
  Auf. Therefore, most absolute sir, if thou wilt have
The leading of thine own revenges, take
The one half of my commission, and set down,
As best thou art experienced, since thou knowst   150
Thy country's strength and weakness, thine own ways,
Whether to knock against the gates of Rome,
Or rudely visit them in parts remote
To fright them ere destroy. But come in;
Let me commend thee first to those that shall   155
Say yea to thy desires. A thousand welcomes!
And more a friend than e'er an enemy;
Yet, Marcius, that was much. Your hand; most wel-
      come!   *Exeunt [Coriolanus and Aufidius].*

[*The two Servingmen come forward.*]

  1. Ser. Here's a strange alteration!   160
  2. Ser. By my hand, I had thought to have strucken
him with a cudgel; and yet my mind gave me his
clothes made a false report of him.
  1. Ser. What an arm he has! He turned me about
with his finger and his thumb, as one would set up a   165
top.
  2. Ser. Nay, I knew by his face that there was something in him; he had, sir, a kind of face, methought
—I cannot tell how to term it.

1. Ser. He had so, looking as it were—Would I 170
were hanged, but I thought there was more in him
than I could think.

2. Ser. So did I, I'll be sworn. He is simply the
rarest man i' the world.

1. Ser. I think he is; but a greater soldier than he 175
you wot on.

2. Ser. Who, my master?

1. Ser. Nay, it's no matter for that.

2. Ser. Worth six on him.

1. Ser. Nay, not so neither; but I take him to be 180
the greater soldier.

2. Ser. Faith, look you, one cannot tell how to say
that; for the defense of a town our general is excellent.

1. Ser. Ay, and for an assault too.   185

[Re-]enter the third Servingman.

3. Ser. O slaves, I can tell you news—news, you
rascals!

Both. What, what, what? Let's partake.

3. Ser. I would not be a Roman, of all nations;
I had as lief be a condemned man.   190

Both. Wherefore? wherefore?

3. Ser. Why, here's he that was wont to thwack
our general—Caius Marcius.

1. Ser. Why do you say "thwack our general"?

3. Ser. I do not say "thwack our general," but he 195
was always good enough for him.

2. Ser. Come, we are fellows and friends. He was

200. **directly:** completely.

201. **scotched:** scored.

202. **carbonado:** piece of meat, scored in preparation for broiling.

203. **An:** if.

204. **broiled:** Alexander Pope's reading; the Folio has "boyld."

206. **made on:** made much of.

209. **bald:** bareheaded.

210. **sanctifies himself with's hand:** holds Coriolanus' hand reverently.

211. **turns up the white o' the eye:** lends admiring attention.

215. **sowl:** seize roughly.

217. **polled:** cropped; cleared.

223. **directitude:** comic error for "discredit."

226. **in blood:** primed for bloodshed. The phrase often has the sense "in first-class physical condition," see I.i.168.

ever too hard for him, I have heard him say so himself.

1. Ser. He was too hard for him directly, to say 200
the troth on't; before Corioli he scotched him and
notched him like a carbonado.

2. Ser. An he had been cannibally given, he might
have broiled and eaten him too.

1. Ser. But more of thy news! 205

3. Ser. Why, he is so made on here within as if
he were son and heir to Mars; set at upper end o' the
table; no question asked him by any of the senators
but they stand bald before him. Our general himself
makes a mistress of him, sanctifies himself with's hand, 210
and turns up the white o' the eye to his discourse. But
the bottom of the news is, our general is cut i' the middle and but one half of what he was yesterday, for the
other has half by the entreaty and grant of the whole
table. He'll go, he says, and sowl the porter of Rome 215
gates by the ears; he will mow all down before him,
and leave his passage polled.

2. Ser. And he's as like to do't as any man I can
imagine.

3. Ser. Do't! He will do't; for look you, sir, he has 220
as many friends as enemies; which friends, sir, as it
were, durst not—look you, sir—show themselves, as we
term it, his friends, whilst he's in directitude.

1. Ser. Directitude? What's that?

3. Ser. But when they shall see, sir, his crest up 225
again and the man in blood, they will out of their burrows, like conies after rain, and revel all with him.

1. Ser. But when goes this forward?

230-31. **parcel:** portion.
238. **vent:** utterance; speech.
243. **cuckolds:** betrayed husbands.

3. *Ser.* Tomorrow; today; presently. You shall have
the drum struck up this afternoon; 'tis as it were a par- 230
cel of their feast, and to be executed ere they wipe
their lips.

2. *Ser.* Why, then we shall have a stirring world
again. This peace is nothing but to rust iron, increase
tailors, and breed ballad-makers.   235

1. *Ser.* Let me have war, say I; it exceeds peace as
far as day does night; it's spritely, waking, audible,
and full of vent. Peace is a very apoplexy, lethargy;
mulled, deaf, sleepy, insensible; a getter of more bas-
tard children than war's a destroyer of men.   240

2. *Ser.* 'Tis so; and as war in some sort may be said
to be a ravisher, so it cannot be denied but peace is
a great maker of cuckolds.

1. *Ser.* Ay, and it makes men hate one another.

3. *Ser.* Reason: because they then less need one an- 245
other. The wars for my money. I hope to see Romans
as cheap as Volscians. They are rising, they are rising.

Both. In, in, in, in!

Exeunt.

[Scene VI. Rome. A public place.]

Enter the two Tribunes, Sicinius and Brutus.

Sic. We hear not of him, neither need we fear him.
His remedies are tame. The present peace
And quietness of the people, which before
Were in wild hurry, here do make his friends
Blush that the world goes well; who rather had,   5

IV. [vi.] 7. **pest'ring:** crowding.

10. **stood to't:** forced the issue of Coriolanus' banishment.

Though they themselves did suffer by't, behold
Dissentious numbers pest'ring streets than see
Our tradesmen singing in their shops, and going
About their functions friendly.

Enter Menenius.

Bru. We stood to't in good time. Is this Menenius?   10
Sic. 'Tis he, 'tis he. O, he is grown most kind
Of late. Hail, sir!
Men.   Hail to you both!
Sic. Your Coriolanus is not much missed
But with his friends. The commonwealth doth stand,   15
And so would do, were he more angry at it.
Men. All's well, and might have been much better if
He could have temporized.
Sic.   Where is he, hear you?
Men. Nay, I hear nothing; his mother and his wife   20
Hear nothing from him.

Enter three or four Citizens.

Cit. The gods preserve you both!
Sic. Godden, our neighbors.
Bru. Godden to you all, godden to you all.
1. Cit. Ourselves, our wives, and children, on our   25
     knees
Are bound to pray for you both.
Sic.   Live and thrive!
Bru. Farewell, kind neighbors; we wished Corio-
     lanus
                                                        30

41. **affecting:** desiring.
56. **horns:** i.e., like a snail.

Had loved you as we did.
   Cit.   Now the gods keep you!
   Both Trib. Farewell, farewell.   *Exeunt Citizens.*
   Sic. This is a happier and more comely time
Than when these fellows ran about the streets   35
Crying confusion.
   Bru.   Caius Marcius was
A worthy officer i' the war, but insolent,
O'ercome with pride, ambitious past all thinking,
Self-loving—   40
   Sic.   And affecting one sole throne,
Without assistance.
   Men.   I think not so.
   Sic. We should by this, to all our lamentation,
If he had gone forth consul, found it so.   45
   Bru. The gods have well prevented it, and Rome
Sits safe and still without him.

Enter an Ædile.

   Æd.   Worthy tribunes,
There is a slave, whom we have put in prison,
Reports the Volsces with two several powers   50
Are ent'red in the Roman territories,
And with the deepest malice of the war
Destroy what lies before 'em.
   Men.   'Tis Aufidius,
Who, hearing of our Marcius' banishment,   55
Thrusts forth his horns again into the world,
Which were inshelled when Marcius stood for Rome,

65. **reason:** discuss.

And durst not once peep out.

  Sic. Come, what talk you of Marcius?

  Bru. Go see this rumorer whipped. It cannot be   60
The Volsces dare break with us.

  Men.   Cannot be!
We have record that very well it can;
And three examples of the like hath been
Within my age. But reason with the fellow   65
Before you punish him, where he heard this,
Lest you shall chance to whip your information
And beat the messenger who bids beware
Of what is to be dreaded.

  Sic.   Tell not me.   70
I know this cannot be.

  Bru.   Not possible.

Enter a Messenger.

  Mess. The nobles in great earnestness are going
All to the Senate House; some news is come
That turns their countenances.   75

  Sic.   'Tis this slave—
Go whip him fore the people's eyes—his raising,
Nothing but his report.

  Mess.   Yes, worthy sir,
The slave's report is seconded, and more,   80
More fearful, is delivered.

  Sic.   What more fearful?

  Mess. It is spoke freely out of many mouths—
How probable I do not know—that Marcius,
Joined with Aufidius, leads a power 'gainst Rome,   85

93. **atone:** reconcile.

109. **whereon you stood:** on which you insisted.

110. **auger's bore:** a small hole such as an auger would make.

And vows revenge as spacious as between
The young'st and oldest thing.
 Sic.   This is most likely!
 Bru. Raised only that the weaker sort may wish
Good Marcius home again.   90
 Sic.   The very trick on't.
 Men. This is unlikely.
He and Aufidius can no more atone
Than violent'st contrariety.

Enter [a second] Messenger.

 2. Mess. You are sent for to the Senate. 95
A fearful army, led by Caius Marcius
Associated with Aufidius, rages
Upon our territories, and have already
O'erborne their way, consumed with fire, and took
What lay before them.   100

Enter Cominius.

 Com. O, you have made good work!
 Men.   What news? What news?
 Com. You have holp to ravish your own daughters
  and
To melt the city leads upon your pates,   105
To see your wives dishonored to your noses—
 Men. What's the news? What's the news?
 Com. Your temples burned in their cement, and
Your franchises, whereon you stood, confined
Into an auger's bore.   110

122. **apron men:** artisans.

123. **voice:** say-so; **occupation:** i.e., the working classes.

126. **Hercules:** a reference to Hercules' gathering of the golden apples of the Hesperides.

134. **constant:** loyal.

Men.   Pray now, your news?
You have made fair work, I fear me. Pray, your news.
If Marcius should be joined wi' the Volscians—
　Com.   If!
He is their god; he leads them like a thing   115
Made by some other deity than Nature,
That shapes man better; and they follow him
Against us brats with no less confidence
Than boys pursuing summer butterflies,
Or butchers killing flies.   120
　Men.   You have made good work,
You and your apron men; you that stood so much
Upon the voice of occupation and
The breath of garlic-eaters!
　Com. He'll shake your Rome about your ears.   125
　Men.   As Hercules
Did shake down mellow fruit. You have made fair
　work!
　Bru. But is this true, sir?
　Com.   Ay; and you'll look pale   130
Before you find it other. All the regions
Do smilingly revolt, and who resists
Are mocked for valiant ignorance,
And perish constant fools. Who is't can blame him?
Your enemies and his find something in him.   135
　Men. We are all undone unless
The noble man have mercy.
　Com.   Who shall ask it?
The tribunes cannot do't for shame; the people
Deserve such pity of him as the wolf   140

158. **clusters:** crowds.

162. **second name of men:** that is, second only to Coriolanus in reputation.

Does of the shepherds; for his best friends, if they
Should say, "Be good to Rome," they charged him
 even
As those should do that had deserved his hate,
And therein showed like enemies.   145
 Men.   'Tis true;
If he were putting to my house the brand
That should consume it, I have not the face
To say, "Beseech you, cease." You have made fair
 hands,   150
You and your crafts! You have crafted fair!
 Com.   You have brought
A trembling upon Rome, such as was never
So incapable of help.
 Both Trib.   Say not we brought it. 155
 Men. How! Was't we? We loved him, but, like
 beasts
And cowardly nobles, gave way unto your clusters,
Who did hoot him out o' the city.
 Com.   But I fear   160
They'll roar him in again. Tullus Aufidius,
The second name of men, obeys his points
As if he were his officer. Desperation
Is all the policy, strength, and defense,
That Rome can make against them.   165

Enter a troop of Citizens.

 Men. Here come the clusters.
And is Aufidius with him? You are they
That made the air unwholesome when you cast

Your stinking greasy caps in hooting at
Coriolanus' exile. Now he's coming,   170
And not a hair upon a soldier's head
Which will not prove a whip; as many coxcombs
As you threw caps up will he tumble down,
And pay you for your voices. 'Tis no matter;
If he could burn us all into one coal,   175
We have deserved it.

Pleb. Faith, we hear fearful news.

1. Cit.   For mine own part,
When I said banish him, I said 'twas pity.

2. Cit. And so did I.   180

3. Cit. And so did I; and, to say the truth, so did
very many of us. That we did, we did for the best;
and though we willingly consented to his banishment, yet it was against our will.

Com. Y'are goodly things, you voices!   185

Men.   You have made
Good work, you and your cry! Shall's to the Capitol?

Com. O, ay, what else?

                    Exeunt [*Cominius and Menenius*].

Sic. Go, masters, get you home; be not dismayed;
These are a side that would be glad to have   190
This true which they so seem to fear. Go home,
And show no sign of fear.

1. Cit. The gods be good to us! Come, masters, let's
home. I ever said we were i' the wrong when we banished him.   195

2. Cit. So did we all. But come, let's home.

                                Exeunt Citizens.

Bru. I do not like this news.

IV. [vii.] 5. dark'ned: overshadowed.
6. **your own:** your own men.
8. **I lame:** i.e., by which I lame.
15. **your particular;** your own sake.

Sic. Nor I.

Bru. Let's to the Capitol. Would half my wealth
Would buy this for a lie!   200

Sic.   Pray let's go.

                                             Exeunt.

[Scene VII. A camp at a short distance from Rome.]

Enter Aufidius with his Lieutenant.

Auf. Do they still fly to the Roman?

Lieut. I do not know what witchcraft's in him, but
Your soldiers use him as the grace fore meat,
Their talk at table, and their thanks at end;
And you are dark'ned in this action, sir,   5
Even by your own.

Auf.   I cannot help it now,
Unless by using means I lame the foot
Of our design. He bears himself more proudlier,
Even to my person, than I thought he would   10
When first I did embrace him; yet his nature
In that's no changeling, and I must excuse
What cannot be amended.

Lieut.   Yet I wish, sir—
I mean, for your particular—you had not   15
Joined in commission with him, but either
Had borne the action of yourself, or else
To him had left it solely.

Auf. I understand thee well; and be thou sure,
When he shall come to his account, he knows not   20
What I can urge against him. Although it seems,

24. **husbandry:** management.

25. **achieve:** conquer.

37. **osprey:** the sea eagle, which preys on fish.

38. **sovereignty of nature:** natural supremacy.

40. **Carry his honors even:** behave so as to retain his honors.

45-6. **not moving/From the casque to the cushion:** not altering from command in war to command in peace. **Casque** (helmet) symbolizes military command, while **cushion** indicates participation in government. See III.[i.]132 and note. Coriolanus is inflexible and unable to adapt his behavior to the requirements of peace.

48. **austerity and garb:** austere manner; a hendiadys.

50. **spices:** dashes; slight touches.

51. **free:** acquit.

52-3. **he has a merit/To choke it in the utt'rance:** his merit should have spoken louder than the fault for which he was banished.

And so he thinks, and is no less apparent
To the vulgar eye, that he bears all things fairly
And shows good husbandry for the Volscian state,
Fights dragonlike, and does achieve as soon   25
As draw his sword; yet he hath left undone
That which shall break his neck or hazard mine
Whene'er we come to our account.

    Lieut. Sir, I beseech you, think you he'll carry
Rome?   30

    Auf. All places yield to him ere he sits down,
And the nobility of Rome are his;
The senators and patricians love him too.
The tribunes are no soldiers, and their people
Will be as rash in the repeal as hasty   35
To expel him thence. I think he'll be to Rome
As is the osprey to the fish, who takes it
By sovereignty of nature. First he was
A noble servant to them, but he could not
Carry his honors even. Whether 'twas pride,   40
Which out of daily fortune ever taints
The happy man; whether defect of judgment,
To fail in the disposing of those chances
Which he was lord of; or whether nature,
Not to be other than one thing, not moving   45
From the casque to the cushion, but commanding
    peace
Even with the same austerity and garb
As he controlled the war; but one of these—
As he hath spices of them all—not all,   50
For I dare so far free him—made him feared,
So hated, and so banished; but he has a merit

55-7. power, unto itself most commendable,/ Hath not a tomb so evident as a chair/T' extol what it hath done: power, a praiseworthy thing in itself, has no greater hazard than the praise it may inspire. Power and popularity are incompatible. Editors have been bothered by the image of power extolling what it hath done on the ground that self-praise is not characteristic of Coriolanus, but praise from any source is meant; it is the people's recognition of his singularity that leads to the hero's downfall.

59. falter: Alexander Dyce's reading; the Folio reads "fouler."

To choke it in the utt'rance. So our virtues
Lie in the interpretation of the time;
And power, unto itself most commendable,   55
Hath not a tomb so evident as a chair
T' extol what it hath done.
One fire drives out one fire; one nail, one nail;
Rights by rights falter, strengths by strengths do fail.
Come, let's away. When, Caius, Rome is thine,   60
Thou art poor'st of all; then shortly art thou mine.

                                               Exeunt.

THE TRAGEDY OF
CORIOLANUS

ACT V

V. Coriolanus seems determined to see his native city destroyed in flames. Cominius makes an unsuccessful plea to him to spare Rome, and Menenius, believing that he can persuade his old friend, also tries and is rejected. Coriolanus, despite boasting to Aufidius that he can never be moved from his loyalty to the Volsces, cannot resist the pleas of his mother, wife, and son. He finally agrees to arrange a truce between the Volsces and Rome. This defection gives Aufidius the opportunity he has wanted. When Coriolanus returns to Antium, assassins coached by Aufidius are at hand. They arouse the populace against Coriolanus, stab him, and trample his body.

‖‖‖‖‖‖‖‖‖‖‖‖‖‖‖‖‖‖‖‖‖‖‖‖‖

V.[i.] 2. Which: who, a common use of the relative pronoun in Elizabethan grammar.

6. coyed: disdained.

ACT V

[Scene I. Rome. A public place.]

*Enter Menenius, Cominius, Sicinius and Brutus, the
two Tribunes, with others.*

Men. No, I'll not go. You hear what he hath said
Which was sometime his general, who loved him
In a most dear particular. He called me father;
But what o' that? Go, you that banished him:
A mile before his tent fall down, and knee   5
The way into his mercy. Nay, if he coyed
To hear Cominius speak, I'll keep at home.
  Com. He would not seem to know me.
  Men.   Do you hear?
  Com. Yet one time he did call me by my name.   10
I urged our old acquaintance, and the drops
That we have bled together. "Coriolanus"
He would not answer to; forbade all names;
He was a kind of nothing, titleless,
Till he had forged himself a name i' the fire   15
Of burning Rome.
  Men.   Why, so! You have made good work,

18. **wracked:** striven.

19. **a noble memory:** a fine thing for which to be remembered.

22. **bare:** empty; lacking in force.

26. **offered:** attempted.

31. **nose:** smell.

34. **brave:** noble.

A pair of tribunes that have wracked for Rome
To make coals cheap—a noble memory!

Com. I minded him how royal 'twas to pardon   20
When it was less expected; he replied,
It was a bare petition of a state
To one whom they had punished.

Men.   Very well.
Could he say less?   25

Com. I offered to awaken his regard
For's private friends; his answer to me was,
He could not stay to pick them in a pile
Of noisome musty chaff. He said 'twas folly,
For one poor grain or two, to leave unburnt   30
And still to nose the offense.

Men.   For one poor grain or two!
I am one of those. His mother, wife, his child,
And this brave fellow too—we are the grains:
You are the musty chaff, and you are smelt   35
Above the moon. We must be burnt for you.

Sic. Nay, pray be patient; if you refuse your aid
In this so never-needed help, yet do not
Upbraid's with our distress. But sure, if you
Would be your country's pleader, your good tongue,   40
More than the instant army we can make,
Might stop our countryman.

Men.   No; I'll not meddle.

Sic. Pray you go to him.

Men.   What should I do?   45

Bru. Only make trial what your love can do
For Rome, towards Marcius.

Men.   Well, and say that Marcius

70. **prove:** try.
71. **Speed how it will:** however it may succeed.

Return me, as Cominius is returned,
Unheard—what then?   50
But as a discontented friend, grief-shot
With his unkindness? Say't be so?

   Sic.   Yet your good will
Must have that thanks from Rome after the measure
As you intended well.   55

   Men.   I'll undertake 't;
I think he'll hear me. Yet to bite his lip
And hum at good Cominius much unhearts me.
He was not taken well: he had not dined;
The veins unfilled, our blood is cold, and then   60
We pout upon the morning, are unapt
To give or to forgive; but when we have stuffed
These pipes and these conveyances of our blood
With wine and feeding we have suppler souls
Than in our priestlike fasts. Therefore I'll watch him   65
Till he be dieted to my request,
And then I'll set upon him.

   Bru. You know the very road into his kindness
And cannot lose your way.

   Men.   Good faith, I'll prove him,   70
Speed how it will. I shall ere long have knowledge
Of my success.   *Exit.*

   Com.   He'll never hear him.

   Sic.   Not?

   Com. I tell you he does sit in gold, his eye   75
Red as 'twould burn Rome, and his injury
The jailer to his pity. I kneeled before him;
'Twas very faintly he said, "Rise"; dismissed me
Thus with his speechless hand. What he would do

80-3. **what he would not,/Bound with an oath to yield to his conditions;/ So that all hope is vain,/Unless his noble mother and his wife:** most editors feel that something is missing in this passage, but the intended sense is probably: "He sent in writing after me details of what he would and would not do, both dependent on our acceding to his conditions, so that the only hope left to us is the solicitation of his mother and wife." **Unless** equals "except."

‖‖‖

V. [ii.] 17. lots to blanks: more than likely.

He sent in writing after me; what he would not,   80
Bound with an oath to yield to his conditions;
So that all hope is vain,
Unless his noble mother and his wife,
Who, as I hear, mean to solicit him
For mercy to his country. Therefore let's hence,   85
And with our fair entreaties haste them on.

Exeunt.

[Scene II. The Volscian camp before Rome.]

Enter Menenius to the Watch on guard.

1. Watch. Stay. Whence are you?
2. Watch.   Stand, and go back.
Men. You guard like men, 'tis well; but, by your
    leave,
I am an officer of state and come   5
To speak with Coriolanus.
1. Watch.   From whence?
Men.   From Rome.
1. Watch. You may not pass; you must return. Our
    general   10
Will no more hear from thence.
    2. Watch. You'll see your Rome embraced with fire
    before
You'll speak with Coriolanus.
Men.   Good my friends,   15
If you have heard your general talk of Rome
And of his friends there, it is lots to blanks
My name hath touched your ears: it is Menenius.

19. **virtue:** power.

22. **lover:** friend.

23. **book:** recorder.

25. **verified:** supported by testimony.

26-7. **with all the size that verity/Would without lapsing suffer:** as largely as possible without lapsing into falsehood.

28. **Like to a bowl upon a subtle ground:** like casting a bowling ball on tricky ground.

30. **stamped the leasing:** authenticated a lie; caused a lie to pass for truth.

37. **factionary on the party:** partial to the cause.

48. **front:** oppose.

1. Watch. Be it so; go back. The virtue of your name
Is not here passable.   20
  Men.   I tell thee, fellow,
Thy general is my lover. I have been
The book of his good acts whence men have read
His fame unparalleled haply amplified;
For I have ever verified my friends,   25
Of whom he's chief, with all the size that verity
Would without lapsing suffer. Nay, sometimes,
Like to a bowl upon a subtle ground,
I have tumbled past the throw, and in his praise
Have almost stamped the leasing; therefore, fellow, 30
I must have leave to pass.

1. Watch. Faith, sir, if you had told as many lies in
his behalf as you have uttered words in your own,
you should not pass here; no, though it were as virtuous to lie as to live chastely. Therefore go back.   35

Men. Prithee, fellow, remember my name is Menenius, always factionary on the party of your general.

2. Watch. Howsoever you have been his liar, as you
say you have, I am one that, telling true under him,
must say you cannot pass. Therefore go back.   40

Men. Has he dined, canst thou tell? For I would not
speak with him till after dinner.

1. Watch. You are a Roman, are you?

Men. I am as thy general is.

1. Watch. Then you should hate Rome, as he does.   45
Can you, when you have pushed out your gates the
very defender of them, and in a violent popular ignorance given your enemy your shield, think to front his

51. **dotant:** man in his dotage; old fool.

58. **estimation:** esteem.

66. **companion:** base fellow, as at IV. [v.] 13-4; **say an errand:** deliver a message. Menenius means that he will deliver in person the word of his arrival which the watch has refused to deliver.

68. **Jack:** knave; **guardant:** on guard.

74. **synod:** assembly.

revenges with the easy groans of old women, the vir-
ginal palms of your daughters, or with the palsied in-   50
tercession of such a decayed dotant as you seem to
be? Can you think to blow out the intended fire your
city is ready to flame in with such weak breath as
this? No, you are deceived; therefore back to Rome
and prepare for your execution. You are condemned;   55
our general has sworn you out of reprieve and pardon.

Men. Sirrah, if thy captain knew I were here, he
would use me with estimation.

1. Watch. Come, my captain knows you not.

Men. I mean thy general.   60

1. Watch. My general cares not for you. Back, I say;
go, lest I let forth your half pint of blood. Back—that's
the utmost of your having. Back.

Men. Nay, but fellow, fellow—

Enter Coriolanus with Aufidius.

Cor. What's the matter?   65

Men. Now, you companion, I'll say an errand for
you; you shall know now that I am in estimation; you
shall perceive that a Jack guardant cannot office me
from my son Coriolanus. Guess but by my entertainment with him if you standst not i' the state of hang-   70
ing, or of some death more long in spectatorship and
crueler in suffering; behold now presently, and swoon
for what's to come upon thee. [*To Coriolanus*] The
glorious gods sit in hourly synod about thy particular
prosperity, and love thee no worse than thy old   75
father Menenius does! O my son! my son! Thou art

88. **servanted:** subject; subordinate.
89. **properly:** personally.
94. **for:** because.
99. **constant temper:** resolute state of mind.
103. **shent:** scolded.

preparing fire for us; look thee, here's water to quench
it. I was hardly moved to come to thee; but, being assured none but myself could move thee, I have been
blown out of your gates with sighs, and conjure thee   80
to pardon Rome and thy petitionary countrymen. The
good gods assuage thy wrath, and turn the dregs of it
upon this varlet here; this, who, like a block, hath
denied my access to thee.

   Cor. Away!   85

   Men. How! Away!

   Cor. Wife, mother, child, I know not. My affairs
Are servanted to others. Though I owe
My revenge properly, my remission lies
In Volscian breasts. That we have been familiar,   90
Ingrate forgetfulness shall poison rather
Than pity note how much. Therefore be gone.
Mine ears against your suits are stronger than
Your gates against my force. Yet, for I loved thee,
Take this along; I writ it for thy sake   95

                            [Gives a letter.]
And would have sent it. Another word, Menenius,
I will not hear thee speak. This man, Aufidius,
Was my beloved in Rome; yet thou beholdst.

   Auf. You keep a constant temper.

               Exeunt [Coriolanus and Aufidius].

   1. Watch. Now, sir, is your name Menenius?   100

   2. Watch. 'Tis a spell, you see, of much power! You
know the way home again.

   1. Watch. Do you hear how we are shent for keep-
ing your greatness back?

V.[iii.] 2. host: army.
  3. plainly: honestly.

2. Watch. What cause, do you think, I have to 105
swoon?

Men. I neither care for the world nor your general;
for such things as you, I can scarce think there's any,
y'are so slight. He that hath a will to die by himself
fears it not from another. Let your general do his 110
worst. For you, be that you are, long; and your misery
increase with your age! I say to you, as I was said to:
Away!   *Exit.*

1. Watch. A noble fellow, I warrant him.

2. Watch. The worthy fellow is our general; he's 115
the rock, the oak not to be wind-shaken.

                                              Exeunt.

[Scene III. The tent of Coriolanus.]

Enter Coriolanus, Aufidius, [and others].

Cor. We will before the walls of Rome tomorrow
Set down our host. My partner in this action,
You must report to the Volscian lords how plainly
I have borne this business.

Auf.   Only their ends   5
You have respected; stopped your ears against
The general suit of Rome; never admitted
A private whisper—no, not with such friends
That thought them sure of you.

Cor.   This last old man,   10
Whom with cracked heart I have sent to Rome,
Loved me above the measure of a father;

13. **godded:** idolized.
17. **grace:** honor.
25. **trunk:** body.

Volumnia pleads with Coriolanus. From Livy, *Decades* (1511).

Nay, godded me indeed. Their latest refuge
Was to send him; for whose old love I have,
Though I showed sourly to him, once more offered 15
The first conditions, which they did refuse
And cannot now accept. To grace him only,
That thought he could do more, a very little
I have yielded to; fresh embassies and suits,
Nor from the state nor private friends, hereafter 20
Will I lend ear to. (*Shout within.*) Ha! What shout is this?
Shall I be tempted to infringe my vow
In the same time 'tis made? I will not.

*Enter, [in mourning habits,] Virgilia, Volumnia,
Valeria, young Marcius, with attendants.*

My wife comes foremost, then the honored mold
Wherein this trunk was framed, and in her hand 25
The grandchild to her blood. But out, affection!
All bond and privilege of nature, break!
Let it be virtuous to be obstinate.
What is that curtsy worth? or those doves' eyes,
Which can make gods forsworn? I melt, and am not 30
Of stronger earth than others. My mother bows,
As if Olympus to a molehill should
In supplication nod; and my young boy
Hath an aspect of intercession which
Great nature cries, "Deny not." Let the Volsces 35
Plow Rome and harrow Italy; I'll never
Be such a gosling to obey instinct, but stand
As if a man were author of himself
And knew no other kin.

45. **out:** i.e., at a loss for words.

50. **the jealous queen of heaven:** Juno, the jealous wife of Jove.

65. **Fillip:** beat; assault.

68. **slight work:** an easy task.

Vir.   My lord and husband!   40
Cor. These eyes are not the same I wore in Rome.
Vir. The sorrow that delivers us thus changed
Makes you think so.
    Cor.   Like a dull actor now
I have forgot my part and I am out,   45
Even to a full disgrace. Best of my flesh,
Forgive my tyranny; but do not say,
For that, "Forgive our Romans." O, a kiss
Long as my exile, sweet as my revenge!
Now, by the jealous queen of heaven, that kiss   50
I carried from thee, dear, and my true lip
Hath virgined it e'er since. You gods! I prate,
And the most noble mother of the world
Leave unsaluted. Sink, my knee, i' the earth; *Kneels.*
Of thy deep duty more impression show   55
Than that of common sons.
    Vol.   O, stand up blest!
Whilst with no softer cushion than the flint
I kneel before thee, and unproperly
Show duty, as mistaken all this while   60
Between the child and parent.   [*Kneels.*]
    Cor.   What's this?
Your knees to me, to your corrected son?
Then let the pebbles on the hungry beach
Fillip the stars; then let the mutinous winds   65
Strike the proud cedars 'gainst the fiery sun,
Murd'ring impossibility, to make
What cannot be slight work.
    Vol.   Thou art my warrior;
I holp to frame thee. Do you know this lady?   70

73. **curdied:** congealed.
75. **epitome:** abstract; referring to his son.
82. **flaw:** tempest.

Cor. The noble sister of Publicola,
The moon of Rome, chaste as the icicle
That's curdied by the frost from purest snow,
And hangs on Dian's temple—dear Valeria!

Vol. This is a poor epitome of yours,   75
Which by the interpretation of full time
May show like all yourself.

Cor.   The god of soldiers,
With the consent of supreme Jove, inform
Thy thoughts with nobleness, that thou mayst prove   80
To shame unvulnerable, and stick i' the wars
Like a great seamark, standing every flaw,
And saving those that eye thee!

Vol.   Your knee, sirrah.

Cor. That's my brave boy.   85

Vol. Even he, your wife, this lady, and myself,
Are suitors to you.

Cor.   I beseech you, peace!
Or, if you'd ask, remember this before:
The thing I have forsworn to grant may never   90
Be held by you denials. Do not bid me
Dismiss my soldiers, or capitulate
Again with Rome's mechanics. Tell me not
Wherein I seem unnatural; desire not
T'allay my rages and revenges with   95
Your colder reasons.

Vol.   O, no more, no more!
You have said you will not grant us anything—
For we have nothing else to ask but that
Which you deny already; yet we will ask,   100
That, if you fail in our request, the blame

106. **bewray:** betray.
112. **Constrains them:** forces them to.
117. **capital:** deadly.
127. **recreant:** traitor.
130. **palm:** symbol of victory.

May hang upon your hardness; therefore hear us.
  Cor. Aufidius, and you Volsces, mark; for we'll
Hear nought from Rome in private. Your request?
  Vol. Should we be silent and not speak, our raiment   105
And state of bodies would bewray what life
We have led since thy exile. Think with thyself
How more unfortunate than all living women
Are we come hither; since that thy sight, which should
Make our eyes flow with joy, hearts dance with com-   110
    forts,
Constrains them weep and shake with fear and sor-
    row,
Making the mother, wife, and child, to see
The son, the husband, and the father, tearing   115
His country's bowels out. And to poor we
Thine enmity's most capital: thou barrest us
Our prayers to the gods, which is a comfort
That all but we enjoy. For how can we,
Alas, how can we for our country pray,   120
Whereto we are bound, together with thy victory,
Whereto we are bound? Alack, or we must lose
The country, our dear nurse, or else thy person,
Our comfort in the country. We must find
An evident calamity, though we had   125
Our wish which side should win; for either thou
Must as a foreign recreant be led
With manacles through our streets, or else
Triumphantly tread on thy country's ruin,
And bear the palm for having bravely shed   130
Thy wife and children's blood. For myself, son,
I purpose not to wait on fortune till

These wars determine; if I cannot persuade thee
Rather to show a noble grace to both parts
Than seek the end of one, thou shalt no sooner   135
March to assault thy country than to tread—
Trust to't, thou shalt not—on thy mother's womb
That brought thee to this world.
   Vir.   Ay, and mine,
That brought you forth this boy to keep your name   140
Living to time.
   Boy.   'A shall not tread on me!
I'll run away till I am bigger, but then I'll fight.
   Cor. Not of a woman's tenderness to be
Requires nor child nor woman's face to see.   145
I have sat too long.   *[Rising.]*
   Vol.   Nay, go not from us thus.
If it were so that our request did tend
To save the Romans, thereby to destroy
The Volsces whom you serve, you might condemn us 150
As poisonous of your honor. No, our suit
Is that you reconcile them: while the Volsces
May say, "This mercy we have showed," the Romans,
"This we received," and each in either side
Give the all-hail to thee, and cry "Be blest   155
For making up this peace!" Thou knowst, great son,
The end of war's uncertain; but this certain,
That if thou conquer Rome the benefit
Which thou shalt thereby reap is such a name
Whose repetition will be dogged with curses;   160
Whose chronicle thus writ: "The man was noble,
But with his last attempt he wiped it out,
Destroyed his country, and his name remains

To the ensuing age abhorred." Speak to me, son.
Thou hast affected the fine strains of honor,   165
To imitate the graces of the gods,
To tear with thunder the wide cheeks o' the air,
And yet to charge thy sulphur with a bolt
That should but rive an oak. Why dost not speak?
Thinkst thou it honorable for a noble man   170
Still to remember wrongs? Daughter, speak you:
He cares not for your weeping. Speak thou, boy;
Perhaps thy childishness will move him more
Than can our reasons. There's no man in the world
More bound to's mother, yet here he lets me prate   175
Like one i' the stocks. Thou hast never in thy life
Showed thy dear mother any courtesy,
When she, poor hen, fond of no second brood,
Has clucked thee to the wars, and safely home
Loaden with honor. Say my request's unjust,   180
And spurn me back; but if it be not so
Thou art not honest, and the gods will plague thee,
That thou restrainst from me the duty which
To a mother's part belongs. He turns away.
Down, ladies; let us shame him with our knees.   185
To his surname Coriolanus 'longs more pride
Than pity to our prayers. Down. An end;
This is the last. So we will home to Rome,
And die among our neighbors. Nay, behold's!
This boy, that cannot tell what he would have   190
But kneels and holds up hands for fellowship,
Does reason our petition with more strength
Than thou hast to deny't. Come, let us go.
This fellow had a Volscian to his mother;

His wife is in Corioli, and his child   195
Like him by chance. Yet give us our dispatch.
I am hushed until our city be afire,
And then I'll speak a little.
                    Holds her by the hand, silent.
    Cor.   O mother, mother!
What have you done? Behold, the heavens do ope,   200
The gods look down, and this unnatural scene
They laugh at. O my mother, mother! O!
You have won a happy victory to Rome;
But for your son—believe it, O, believe it!—
Most dangerously you have with him prevailed,   205
If not most mortal to him. But let it come.
Aufidius, though I cannot make true wars,
I'll frame convenient peace. Now, good Aufidius,
Were you in my stead, would you have heard
A mother less, or granted less, Aufidius?   210
    Auf. I was moved withal.
    Cor.   I dare be sworn you were!
And, sir, it is no little thing to make
Mine eyes to sweat compassion. But, good sir,
What peace you'll make, advise me. For my part,   215
I'll not to Rome, I'll back with you; and pray you
Stand to me in this cause. O mother! Wife!
    Auf. [*Aside*] I am glad thou hast set thy mercy and
        thy honor
At difference in thee. Out of that I'll work   220
Myself a former fortune.
    Cor. [*To the ladies*] Ay, by and by;
But we will drink together; and you shall bear

V.[iv.] 8. **stay upon:** await.

10. **condition:** character.

17. **horse:** that is, than a horse remembers its dam.

A better witness back than words, which we,
On like conditions, will have countersealed.   225
Come, enter with us. Ladies, you deserve
To have a temple built you. All the swords
In Italy, and her confederate arms,
Could not have made this peace.

                                    Exeunt.

[Scene IV. Rome. A public place.]

Enter Menenius and Sicinius.

Men. See you yond coign o' the Capitol, yond cor-
nerstone?

Sic. Why, what of that?

Men. If it be possible for you to displace it with
your little finger, there is some hope the ladies of   5
Rome, especially his mother, may prevail with him.
But I say there is no hope in't; our throats are sentenced, and stay upon execution.

Sic. Is't possible that so short a time can alter the
condition of a man?   10

Men. There is differency between a grub and a butterfly; yet your butterfly was a grub. This Marcius is
grown from a man to dragon; he has wings, he's more
than a creeping thing.

Sic. He loved his mother dearly.   15

Men. So did he me; and he no more remembers his
mother now than an eight-year-old horse. The tartness
of his face sours ripe grapes; when he walks, he moves

19. **engine:** war machine.
20. **corselet:** body armor.
22. **state:** chair of state; **as a thing made for Alexander:** like an image of Alexander the Great.
37. **hale:** haul.

like an engine and the ground shrinks before his
treading. He is able to pierce a corselet with his eye,   20
talks like a knell, and his hum is a battery. He sits in
his state as a thing made for Alexander. What he bids
be done is finished with his bidding. He wants nothing
of a god but eternity, and a heaven to throne in.

Sic. Yes—mercy, if you report him truly.   25

Men. I paint him in the character. Mark what mercy
his mother shall bring from him. There is no more
mercy in him than there is milk in a male tiger; that
shall our poor city find. And all this is 'long of you.

Sic. The gods be good unto us!   30

Men. No, in such a case the gods will not be good
unto us. When we banished him we respected not
them; and, he returning to break our necks, they respect not us.

Enter a Messenger.

Mess. Sir, if you'd save your life, fly to your house.   35
The plebeians have got your fellow tribune
And hale him up and down; all swearing if
The Roman ladies bring not comfort home
They'll give him death by inches.

Enter another Messenger.

Sic.   What's the news?   40
2. *Mess.* Good news, good news! The ladies have
    prevailed,

S.D. after l. 51. **hautboys:** oboes.

52. **sackbuts:** instruments resembling trombones; **psalteries:** stringed instruments similar to the zither.

The Volscians are dislodged, and Marcius gone.
A merrier day did never yet greet Rome,
No, not the expulsion of the Tarquins.   45
  Sic.   Friend,
Art thou certain this is true? Is't most certain?
  2. Mess. As certain as I know the sun is fire.
Where have you lurked, that you make doubt of it?
Ne'er through an arch so hurried the blown tide   50
As the recomforted through the gates. Why, hark you!
      Trumpets, hautboys, drums beat, all together.
The trumpets, sackbuts, psalteries, and fifes,
Tabors and cymbals, and the shouting Romans,
Make the sun dance. Hark you!   *A shout within.*
  Men.   This is good news.   55
I will go meet the ladies. This Volumnia
Is worth of consuls, senators, patricians,
A city full; of tribunes such as you,
A sea and land full. You have prayed well today:
This morning for ten thousand of your throats   60
I'd not have given a doit. Hark, how they joy!
              Sound still with the shouts.
  Sic. First, the gods bless you for your tidings; next,
Accept my thankfulness.
  2. Mess.   Sir, we have all
Great cause to give thanks.   65
  Sic.   They are near the city?
  Mess. Almost at point to enter.
  Sic.   We'll meet them,
And help the joy.
                       Exeunt.

V. [vi.] 8. purge: clear.

[Scene V. Rome. A street near the gate.]

Enter two Senators with Ladies, [Volumnia, Virgilia, Valeria,] passing over the stage, with other Lords.

1. Sen. Behold our patroness, the life of Rome!
Call all your tribes together, praise the gods,
And make triumphant fires; strew flowers before them.
Unshout the noise that banished Marcius,
Repeal him with the welcome of his mother;   5
Cry "Welcome, ladies, welcome!"
   All.   Welcome, ladies, welcome!
   A flourish with drums and trumpets. [Exeunt.]

[Scene VI. Antium. A public place.]

Enter Tullus Aufidius, with attendants.

Auf. Go tell the lords o' the city I am here;
Deliver them this paper; having read it,
Bid them repair to the market place, where I,
Even in theirs and in the commons' ears,
Will vouch the truth of it. Him I accuse   5
The city ports by this hath entered and
Intends t' appear before the people, hoping
To purge himself with words. Dispatch.
               [Exeunt attendants.]

15-6. wherein/You wished us parties: to which you wished us to be party.

24-5. admits/A good construction: permits a favorable interpretation.

Enter three or four Conspirators of Aufidius' faction.

Most welcome!
  1. Con.   How is it with our general?   **10**
  Auf.   Even so
As with a man by his own alms empoisoned,
And with his charity slain.
  2. Con.   Most noble sir,
If you do hold the same intent wherein   **15**
You wished us parties, we'll deliver you
Of your great danger.
  Auf.   Sir, I cannot tell;
We must proceed as we do find the people.
  3. Con. The people will remain uncertain whilst **20**
'Twixt you there's difference; but the fall of either
Makes the survivor heir of all.
  Auf.   I know it;
And my pretext to strike at him admits
A good construction. I raised him, and I pawned **25**
Mine honor for his truth; who being so heightened,
He watered his new plants with dews of flattery,
Seducing so my friends; and to this end
He bowed his nature, never known before
But to be rough, unswayable, and free.   **30**
  3. Con. Sir, his stoutness
When he did stand for consul, which he lost
By lack of stooping—
  Auf. That I would have spoke of.
Being banished for't, he came unto my hearth, **35**
Presented to my knife his throat. I took him;

39. **files:** lists; ranks of soldiers.

42. **Which he did end all his:** which was wholly his in the end.

45-6. **waged me with his countenance as if/I had been mercenary:** i.e., patronized me as though I were only a hired soldier.

52. **my sinews shall be stretched upon him:** I shall exert every effort to his destruction.

53. **rheum:** moisture; tears.

57. **post:** i.e., a mere messenger.

63. **vantage:** opportunity.

Made him joint servant with me; gave him way
In all his own desires; nay, let him choose
Out of my files, his projects to accomplish,
My best and freshest men; served his designments   40
In mine own person; holp to reap the fame
Which he did end all his, and took some pride
To do myself this wrong. Till, at the last,
I seemed his follower, not partner; and
He waged me with his countenance as if   45
I had been mercenary.

   1. Con.   So he did, my lord.
The army marveled at it; and, in the last,
When he had carried Rome, and that we looked
For no less spoil than glory—   50

   Auf.   There was it;
For which my sinews shall be stretched upon him.
At a few drops of women's rheum, which are
As cheap as lies, he sold the blood and labor
Of our great action; therefore shall he die,   55
And I'll renew me in his fall. But, hark!

Drums and trumpets sound, with great shouts of the
                      people.

   1. Con. Your native town you entered like a post,
And had no welcomes home; but he returns
Splitting the air with noise.

   2. Con.   And patient fools,   60
Whose children he hath slain, their base throats tear
With giving him glory.

   3. Con.   Therefore, at your vantage,
Ere he express himself or move the people

66. **along:** prone; i.e., when he has been struck down.

67-8. **After your way his tale pronounced shall bury/His reasons with his body:** after you have told his story in your own fashion, any justification he might have made will be buried with him.

78. **easy fines:** light punishment.

80-1. **answering us/With our own charge:** returning us no gain, merely what we had originally supplied him with.

With what he would say, let him feel your sword,   65
Which we will second. When he lies along,
After your way his tale pronounced shall bury
His reasons with his body.
    Auf.   Say no more:
Here come the lords.   70

Enter the Lords of the city.

    Lords. You are most welcome home.
    Auf.   I have not deserved it.
But, worthy lords, have you with heed perused
What I have written to you?
    Lords.   We have.   75
    1. Lord. And grieve to hear't.
What faults he made before the last, I think
Might have found easy fines; but there to end
Where he was to begin, and give away
The benefit of our levies, answering us   80
With our own charge, making a treaty where
There was a yielding—this admits no excuse.
    Auf. He approaches; you shall hear him.

*Enter Coriolanus, marching with drum and colors;
    the Commoners being with him.*

    Cor. Hail, lords! I am returned your soldier;
No more infected with my country's love   85
Than when I parted hence, but still subsisting
Under your great command. You are to know

97. **compounded:** agreed.
109. **drops of salt:** i.e., tears.

That prosperously I have attempted, and
With bloody passage led your wars even to
The gates of Rome. Our spoils we have brought home   90
Doth more than counterpoise a full third part
The charges of the action. We have made peace
With no less honor to the Antiates
Than shame to the Romans; and we here deliver,
Subscribed by the consuls and patricians,   95
Together with the seal o' the Senate, what
We have compounded on.

Auf.   Read it not, noble lords;
But tell the traitor in the highest degree
He hath abused your powers.   100

  Cor. Traitor! How now?

  Auf.   Ay, traitor, Marcius.

  Cor..   Marcius!

  Auf. Ay, Marcius, Caius Marcius! Dost thou think
I'll grace thee with that robbery, thy stol'n name   105
Coriolanus, in Corioli?
You lords and heads o' the state, perfidiously
He has betrayed your business and given up,
For certain drops of salt, your city Rome—
I say your city—to his wife and mother;   110
Breaking his oath and resolution like
A twist of rotten silk; never admitting
Counsel o' the war; but at his nurse's tears
He whined and roared away your victory,
That pages blushed at him, and men of heart   115
Looked wond'ring each at others.

  Cor.   Hearst thou, Mars?

125. **notion:** understanding.
137. **blind fortune:** sheer luck.

Auf. Name not the god, thou boy of tears—
Cor.   Ha!
Auf.   —no more. 120
  Cor. Measureless liar, thou hast made my heart
Too great for what contains it. "Boy"! O slave!
Pardon me, lords, 'tis the first time that ever
I was forced to scold. Your judgments, my grave lords,
Must give this cur the lie; and his own notion—   125
Who wears my stripes impressed upon him, that
Must bear my beating to his grave—shall join
To thrust the lie unto him.
  1. Lord. Peace, both, and hear me speak.
  Cor. Cut me to pieces, Volsces; men and lads,   130
Stain all your edges on me. "Boy"! False hound!
If you have writ your annals true, 'tis there
That, like an eagle in a dovecote, I
Fluttered your Volscians in Corioli.
Alone I did it. "Boy"!   135
  Auf.   Why, noble lords,
Will you be put in mind of his blind fortune,
Which was your shame, by this unholy braggart,
Fore your own eyes and ears?
  Conspirators.   Let him die for't.   140
  All People. Tear him to pieces.—Do it presently.—
He killed my son.—My daughter.—He killed my
cousin Marcus.—He killed my father.
  2. Lord. Peace, ho! No outrage! Peace!
The man is noble, and his fame folds in   145
This orb o' the earth. His last offenses to us
Shall have judicious hearing. Stand, Aufidius,

And trouble not the peace.

Cor.   O that I had him,
With six Aufidiuses, or more—his tribe,   150
To use my lawful sword!

Auf.   Insolent villain!

Conspirators. Kill, kill, kill, kill, kill him!

The Conspirators draw and kill Coriolanus, who falls.
Aufidius stands on him.

Lords.   Hold, hold, hold, hold!

Auf. My noble masters, hear me speak.   155

1. Lord.   O Tullus!

2. Lord. Thou hast done a deed whereat valor will
weep.

3. Lord. Tread not upon him. Masters all, be quiet;
Put up your swords.   160

Auf. My lords, when you shall know—as in this rage,
Provoked by him, you cannot—the great danger
Which this man's life did owe you, you'll rejoice
That he is thus cut off. Please it your honors
To call me to your Senate, I'll deliver   165
Myself your loyal servant, or endure
Your heaviest censure.

1. Lord.   Bear from hence his body,
And mourn you for him. Let him be regarded
As the most noble corse that ever herald   170
Did follow to his urn.

2. Lord.   His own impatience
Takes from Aufidius a great part of blame.
Let's make the best of it.

Auf.   My rage is gone,   175
And I am struck with sorrow. Take him up.

Help, three o' the chiefest soldiers; I'll be one.
Beat thou the drum, that it speak mournfully;
Trail your steel pikes. Though in this city he
Hath widowed and unchilded many a one,   180
Which to this hour bewail the injury,
Yet he shall have a noble memory.
Assist.

> *Exeunt, bearing the body of Coriolanus.*
> *A dead march sounded.*